Lucy works in Telesales

SIMON BELL

"You can sell anything if you identify the customer's emotional connection with what you are selling. If you do, the added bonus is that the customer will enjoy buying from you and then do it again regularly."

Published by Sales Call Expert publishing

Published by Sales Call Expert publishing
Wessex House, Wessex Close, Christchurch, Dorset BH23 4SS

www.salescallexpert.com | 0845 423 0423

Design and photography by Orbital Design
www.orbital.co.uk

ISBN 978-0-9567634-0-2

This book is proudly printed on paper which contains wood from a sustainable source.

Contents

Foreword

This book is dedicated to my daughters who will soon be entering the world of work, job, career and PAYE.

When Tony Blair uttered those immortal words, "Education, Education, Education," all I heard was 'Tax, Tax, Tax," and to me, the over-proceduralisation of our workplace was complete.

Anyone with a job these days is essentially run by an accountant to the point that their personality is of little value. The working day becomes a chore and Friday night is a release from the servitude and this release is often expressed as binge drinking.

Lucy works in Telesales is a novel about a pretty young female who finishes her degree and enters the world of work in a dismal economic environment.

Many of our everyday trials and tribulations are exposed and solved through the eyes of a sweet, innocent and well-meaning human being who is only truly happy when everyone around her is happy too.

All the characters in the book are real but I have changed the names and mixed up the circumstances to conceal their identities.

I want to thank everyone who has helped me develop my ideas to this point. I know I can be a pain and I am sorry if I have offended you but what we did together was essential and hopefully, you gained something from the experience. Fortunately, most people who have helped me have really enjoyed the process – or at least, that is what they tell me.

Introduction

I have been in sales for a long time, since birth in 1964 actually. If I smiled, gurgled and waved my chubby arms around, I was treated like royalty. More recently, if I smile at the barister serving my coffee, I can taste the care and attention.

We are selling ourselves all the time and our sales pitch is represented by the way we walk, dress, look and act. We always strive for the best deal and choose our significant other accordingly.

This social valuation is of paramount importance when selling on the phone and our value is represented by the sound of our voice. Unfortunately, we often sound robotic because we have been programmed by our employers, schools and environment. We do not understand how to present ourselves when the only thing that matters is sound because we are unfamiliar with the rules when status, image and physiology are excluded.

It took me many years to realise that I was different. My poor eyesight went unrecognised for nearly nine years of my life. I remember the teacher demanding that I read what was on the blackboard but all I could see was a grey wash. She made me come to the front of the class and suddenly, standing so close, we realised that I needed glasses.

They say that children with poor eyesight become social mappers. They have to, otherwise they would get into all sorts of difficulties and I learned to live my life by my ears, listening to every intonation, sigh and shift in order to predict others' behaviour.

There is a whole world of minute sounds that most people do not realise exists because they don't have to, they can see. This world is subject to a special set of rules that are of fundamental importance during telephone sales.

Unfortunately, you cannot simply learn the rules and apply them. You have to adopt them and that means a different way of acting, a brave way that requires you to put aside conventional thinking and be prepared for anything, any behaviour and any opinion.

People are so different when you really start to understand them and it is this uniqueness that makes telephone selling such fun.

It doesn't matter what you think, know or even believe. What matters is what they (your customers) want to hear.

There are essentially five rules that will help you identify what they want to hear; but to adopt these rules you have to be prepared for change. Most good telephone sales training is all about your attitude and your behaviour because that has a direct effect on others' attitudes and behaviour, which is all represented by the sound of the human voice.

I have named the first eighteen chapters of this book after core human emotions because I want to introduce you to the sounds that drive our behaviour; and every chapter is stuffed with learning about how to optimise your interaction with everyone you call and meet.

Primarily, I hope that you enjoy Lucy's story but I also hope that I have made it evident how she responds to the immediate world around her. These reactions are essential for her adoption of the rules and tools she applies to her telephone sales, allowing her to put emotionally-enriched customers first and therefore make a lot more money.

If you have any comments about her behaviour at work or think that Lucy would benefit from working in your industry, then please contact me.

“Oh dear”

she said and
you could hear
the shame in
her voice but
the decision
was necessary.

1. Shame

"Awwww." She felt dreadful. Four days and nights of drinking was obviously too much for her. It was supposed to be fun, a laugh, a release from the tunnel vision required to maximise her chances of a good degree.

Her single bed was warm and cosy, soft and sweet-smelling from Red Bull but the room in her shared house was freezing; it always was in the morning. During the winter there had been ice on the inside of the windows.

Had she really told Jack it was over? Yes, in a blazing row, something inside her that wouldn't be numbed by the alcohol kept telling her that she had to 'get on'. A week of after-exam activities was fine but when these activities were mainly an excuse for drinking, well, that wasn't fine in her plan. At five foot five and eight and half stone with very little puppy fat, Lucy was built like a fairy but her body language told the onlooker that she was a fairy not to be messed with. She always wanted to experience new things but would easily stop when she calculated that they didn't suit her any longer.

"Do you want some tea?" shouted Pauline through Lucy's closed door. Lucy knew it was less of a kind offer and more of a demand to get up. Today was Pauline's event. They were going to Brighton to 'see the rock' and it was the thinnest excuse for another day and night of drinking. Lucy had been giving Pauline bad vibes about this all day yesterday at Alton Towers. Something inside her had been preparing the ground to get out of this stupidity. It wasn't like any of them had any money. They were all extracting the last of their student loans and fourteen thousand, eight hundred and twenty five pounds was quite enough borrowing for Lucy.

She had kept her overdraft at a minimum by working as floor manager in a local bistro for three nights a week. Her social life had suffered but somehow she made up for it during the day. As a student, her strength had been that she didn't need the usual quantity of alcohol to be herself and now she wasn't a student. She had finished her final exams and their tenancy ran out on Sunday so she had four days to get the ball rolling. She knew that if she didn't, her mum would fuss and take over, coming up with ridiculous options like helping out at the stables or assisting at the rescue centre. She would fuss anyway and that is why Lucy planned to stay with her dad instead. He would only pity her for having no options and that was bad enough.

"No thanks, I don't feel well," she shouted back to Pauline. "What?" demanded Pauline. "But you are coming today, right?" Lucy really didn't feel well, she had started to shake with what she wanted to believe was alcohol poisoning. She hoped it wasn't but she allowed the shakes to come on as Pauline scowled at her around her door. Lucy knew that scowl; it meant that Pauline was determined to have her way and Lucy had never dared to cross her when she was in that mood. She assumed that Pauline would end their friendship if ever she did. But Lucy wasn't doing another day of drinking and if Pauline was prepared to put her health at risk, well, then she was no friend at all. "I'm sorry" she said, "but look at me." She pulled her duvet aside and showed Pauline her shaking body. "I am not well. You know I can't take drink like you can." This mild compliment softened Pauline a little and Lucy took advantage of the moment. "Would you mind getting me some tablets?" A moment of indecision crossed Pauline's face and she concluded triumphantly: "I can't, I have to meet the bus and round everyone up. You'll have to manage on your own." "Okay, fine, you have a good time today," Lucy said in a voice that was meant to convey that she was gutted to miss out.

To be fair, she would have been delighted to join in if she felt on top form, hadn't done the same thing for four days previously, had the money and didn't need to get a job. But she did and she knew her mum would have done the same, her dad would be proud of her, her sister would remain jealous and her best friend would have been delighted for her. She wasn't sure what Jack would think. Did it matter? It did. Lucy hoped to see him again and convince him that she just needed to sort out her next step. It was okay for him because his dad had organised a year's placement abroad for him with some oceanographic team.

When she wasn't quite sure what to do she often asked herself: "What would the five year old me say?" And the answer was always the same: "Get on and make the best of what you have."

As a child she had been effervescent, enlivening any gathering of people, breaking the ice, bringing people out of themselves and extracting valuable opinions from the most unusual candidates. The adult world had rationalised this behaviour but deep down she knew something really exciting was just around the corner and she, Lucy, was going to embrace it with wide open arms.

AUTHOR'S NOTE

Lucy has stayed open to new ideas for as long as she can remember. By playing someone else's game she has gained new knowledge and a better understanding of herself but the time has come for her to do things her own way. Others may not be happy with her decision but if they have any value to her, they will accept that she needs to get on.

“Phew!”

Just by thinking it she feels relieved and looks forward to the results.

2. Relief

As Pauline slammed the front door, Lucy was satisfied that the agenda was set. Today was dedicated to starting her job hunting and that was good but, she was just going to allow herself a couple of hours of deep sleep before she got on.

Uh, oh. Twelve noon. She had slept for three hours. "I obviously needed it," she thought but it was later than she had planned to start. "Urgh." She did feel dreadful but planned to eat and drink something, get dressed and buy some pills and with that set in her mind, she found she could function through the pain in her head, stomach and legs.

Her dad had bought her a really cosy dressing gown and she was grateful for it now. She pulled up the collar, tightened the soft belt and pushed her feet into the flip flops she used as slippers. In the kitchen there wasn't a mug unused but as she grasped her favourite, intending to give it a swill, her stomach lurched, telling her that coffee would be too acidic today. She popped some bread into the toaster but as she planned what to spread on it, her mouth made it clear that 'plain' should be the theme for this morning. The bread popped up warm and crispy soft. Memories of fat sausages rolled in hot, soft, butter-oozing bread came to mind and it took a lot of will power to hold back her bile. Feeling glum she chewed on her bread and drank her tap water but she couldn't get further than the first slow swallow. Even moving away from her spot in the kitchen was a challenge.

Pills were needed and by visualising their diversionary effect, she balanced through the dressing procedure. Fresh underwear always made her feel better and a simple cotton dress was the compromise between ease of procedure and image. However ill she may feel, at twenty three, she didn't want to miss a moment of attention that her role in society commanded. There were two cctv cameras on her walk to the corner shop and she was never going to give those fat old farts who she assumed manned the control desk the satisfaction of knowing that she wasn't on top form.

Simply standing in air that was moving, alive on her doorstep, made her feel better. But the sun was bright so she slipped back in and borrowed a pair of Pauline's shades from the mantelpiece. Walking was easy but it was odd to even think that. Walking perfectly upright was a struggle but she made herself do it, conscious of how she looked on the camera above the bus stop. "Am I myself if I am not literally being myself?" she pondered silently and focussed on the implications of being who we thought it was best to be.

As she entered the shop she put on her cold face, partly for the camera blatantly pointing at her on entry but partly because 'the Corner Shop' could be the best and worst of shopping experiences. Mr Patel, or 'Mean Bob' as everyone called him, was only interested in how much you spent versus the time you took to spend it. He would look through you and make no comment as he watched a basket fill up. If it was less than half full at the counter he would make comments like "chocolate pudding goes well with custard" and "you shouldn't drink wine without potato snacks." Shoppers new to this experience would act on his suggestions, somehow believing his opinion to be sensible and caring advice; but once you knew that he didn't give a fig for anything but his own pocket, it became a bit of a game to buy things that would prompt suggestions that could be ignored – much to his annoyance. Luckily, today, his wife, Rita, was at the till and her warm smile could have been prescribed on the NHS. Lucy felt better immediately but her instant improvement didn't fool Rita. Just telling the caring, homely lady all about her plan that morning made a one hundred percent difference and Lucy walked away with fresh bread, fruit, soup and a magazine to supplement her job hunt.

Doing it online was the only way these days. All wisdom pointed towards a double dip recession and even a good degree in languages wouldn't get her a position relevant to her studies at a reputable organisation. The big boys had done the rounds of the universities but they had naturally picked off those who had been predicted first class degrees and Lucy was predicted a two:two – a fact she wasn't proud of, but the second year had been such fun. In her heart she knew that a two:one was her destiny but right now she was a hung-over student who hadn't even started looking for her first real job. At least she was a few days ahead of her friends who would already be into the tenth vodka or can of the day.

The pills were enough to fool her body into eating some of the bread and soup and the pointless tittle-tattle of the magazine, blended with her wholesome chat with Rita, put her in the mood for action.

It was easy to click options and she soon populated the sections about attitude to work, sport and lifestyle. This is what she knew she knew but when it came to applying herself to a role, well, how could she know? "I can't know what I don't know," she said aloud.

A website suggested that she imagine herself in a role at work but administration was the only image that she could conjure, partly because that is what she felt she had done for the past three years by studying. "But I don't want a sedentary role at work," she thought. Lucy had become used to the broken schedule of lectures. She would cycle to class in the morning, back for lunch and out again for an afternoon session, sometimes doing it again if someone good was playing at the student union that night. Three miles was a long walk – especially in heels – but an easy cycle ride; and as she rarely got trashed, she was relatively safe on the roads at 3am. Of course, she often stayed with Jack who was closer to town but he liked completely different music, more mainstream and less ethnic than Lucy's favourites.

Her other options seemed to be the care profession, but she had always shivered at the thought of another person's waste products; or, sales. She wouldn't lower herself to that so she clicked away. Having registered with three online job sites and a local recruitment agency, her day was done. Her head was back to normal and her body had converted her feeling of illness to that of fatigue.

Crash. The front door smashed open. "Hellooo," shouted Pauline, with several others. They were well oiled and struggled to stand but Pauline hugged Lucy and said that she hoped she was well; so,

Lucy made them all a cup of tea, which they drank with her bread and some honey. In front of the telly they mumbled stories about mooning on the bus, getting ripped off by fish and chip restaurants and swimming in the sea with their clothes on but soon subsided into snoring; so Lucy turned off the telly and went to bed, glad to have used her day in a more productive manner.

AUTHOR'S NOTE

Lucy would be worried that she has taken on too much if she didn't feel so rough. Her career is a huge project and she hardly knows where to start but she recognises that just doing something is enough to get her going. So, she breaks the whole down into smaller tasks to maintain her enthusiasm and by visualising the end result, she manages to enjoy the process too.

Denial can be a useful planning tool

Looking down seemed to be the right response while she mumbled

"Sorry,"

knowing the feeling would pass.

3. Guilt

They were all in the kitchen, drinking tea and eating toast and Marmite, when she came down next morning.

Today was the first of five that didn't even attempt to cover up a big drinking session. It was a tour of the town's pubs, starting at eleven; and there were thirty six pubs! Lucy was cheerful. She felt good after a day off the alcohol and making a start at her job search. She chatted easily about their day in Brighton but they were suffering from prolonged debauchery and were not really making sense. Josh and his new girlfriend Kerry were on best form, mainly because they had been snogging on the bus which reduced their drinking time. They had split from the group on arrival and had lunch in The Lanes before they strolled around the hippy shops.

Matty, Johno and Russell were really suffering and not speaking a lot. They had competed on every drink, starting with cans on the bus, moving to pints in the pub and spirits in the clubs. They had even carried on with a bottle of vodka in the bus on the way home. Russell said that all they needed was to get drinking again and then they would be fine. Lucy wasn't sure that Johno would make it for a whole day and she wondered if it was a type of insecurity that made them do it.

"So," said Pauline, "are you ready then, Lucy?" "Grrr," thought Lucy. You're going to make me say this again aren't you? "No, I'm not coming," she said. There was a stunned silence. Pauline smirked and waited. It was Matty who challenged her. "But we agreed to do this week of activities together," he said, looking her straight in the eye. Lucy gulped. She knew she had agreed but she had had enough. What was the point of it? But how could she get out of it without looking bad? "I know I agreed but, yesterday taught me something," she conceded. "I can't take my alcohol like you guys. Plus, I need to find a job and earn some money to pay off this horrible loan. Don't you guys worry about that?" she asked, moving the emphasis to them and the hated student loan.

Pauline had a position at her dad's company in London. It was only as office junior and it wasn't really a job but it was something and it was money, so she stayed silent. The others looked glum. They knew they had to do something about it but wanted to put off the inevitable rejection for as long as possible. Everyone they knew was taking handouts from their parents too and only a handful had secured work, nearly all voluntary. "So, I'm not joining you to spend money that I don't have just to destroy my liver and brain cells," she concluded. More silence followed but her work was done; so she made herself more tea in silence and offered more to the others, but no one accepted.

She blew on the rim of her cup, hoping for an end to the guilt she was feeling. "Come on then," announced Pauline. "We said we would meet the others in The Crown at eleven," and off they went, leaving Lucy with a few 'see ya's" and "catch yer laters."

"Oh, well." she thought. "We will all be moving on soon and I am determined to make the best of these new opportunities."

Her inbox was empty so she decided to go for a run.

Her long legs looked great in her short running shorts and the tight top complimented her slim physique. Her trainers were old but she had learned to run on her toes anyway. Her preference was to go fast over a short distance and today she flew around her route, fuelled by caffeine and a week of doing no exercise.

The adrenaline rush drove her on to tidy her room, vacuum the house, take a shower, put on her tracksuit and make another cup of tea in readiness for business. It was surprising how pleased she was that the others were all out drinking themselves silly while she was growing and improving. It made her growth even more valuable and put her in the right frame of mind for success.

Divide and rule

AUTHOR'S NOTE

Lucy doesn't want to be influenced by group behaviour. She recognises that the leaders may not be concerned for her welfare but she doesn't want to be branded a troublemaker. By identifying allies in the group, she is able to do her own thing without any loss of face while the group focuses on retaining the others that might leave too.

“Ooh,
that’s nice,”

knowing the future
is bright.

4. Surprise

"Hello, may I speak to Lynne Thompson please?" Lucy was using her best business telephone manner. It felt a little pompous but she had seen her mum do something similar and she didn't know how else to go about the call. An email had invited her to call Lynne with reference to her application to the local recruitment company. "Ms Thompson speaking," came the reply. "Yes, hello," said Lucy. "Your email suggested I call because I made an application and I think I would be really good at lots of things because I have just finished my degree and I am very keen to learn and really need the money." "Hold on dear," interrupted Ms Thompson. "I will tell you how this works and that means you respond to my questions, are we clear?"

Lucy blushed and went all hot. She was so embarrassed but remembered how determined she was so replied, "Yes, I understand." "Good," said Ms Thompson. "Do you have any experience of work?" "Yes," said Lucy. "What work?" spat Ms Thompson. "I worked as a floor manager at Amalfi Bistro for three nights a week for three years," she said. "Oh dear, the whole world wants to work in food retailing these days," said Ms Thompson. "What other skills do you have?" "Errr, none" said Lucy. "Well, you clearly like to talk so we should try you in sales."

Lucy was delighted. She hadn't in her wildest dreams expected a 'yes' so fast. This was her first call and she was being offered a salary starting on Monday. All training would be given and after the induction period, she would be offered a commission which could double her salary if she was any good.

She put down the phone and immediately thought that she might join the others but instead, packed some sandwiches in her backpack and walked to the Downs, buying a can of Diet Coke on the way. "Hold on a minute," she thought. The excitement of the moment had worn off. "I don't want to work in sales." Everyone she knew thought sales was a dirty profession, if you could even call it a profession. All the salesmen she had ever come across were bullies, pushing their wide screen TVs, utilities or Mean Bob suggesting potato snacks.

She had no respect for any of them at all. Did she really want to be branded with the same bad attitude? Could she tell her friends? Her mum? It was all too much. She knew she couldn't handle such a social decline. What if she couldn't get her real career going when the economy picked up? She had to get on the phone and find a proper job.

Having an offer already, gave her great confidence. Now she was a sales person looking to further her career. Okay, so she hadn't yet worked in sales. How difficult could it be? Plus, she would soon have a languages degree and even a two:two had to count for something these days.

Fifty thousand pounds per annum was the lowest salary on offer in most of the broadsheets but at twenty three, Lucy didn't feel ready to command those heady heights. The tabloids were a little more accessible but most positions on offer were in care or shops.

There was nothing in the food or entertainment sections except for chefs and she wasn't at all qualified for that. The most complicated food Lucy had ever prepared was pasta with sauce and fried chicken – oh, and crusty bread – and that was extravagant for her. She mostly lived off baked potatoes, cheese and garlic bread. The modern culture of food made her quite angry. So many 'so called' chefs raced around to ruin food with adornments that prevented you tasting the actual meat and/or vegetables. That, combined with so much hype about obesity, was enough to enrage anyone with a drop of common sense. At least it stopped her wasting time watching the cooking programmes that the television schedulers were so fond of these days.

There were quite a few positions for skilled tradesmen but she didn't have a trade and she wasn't even going to waste her time asking about the work from home scams.

The local paper offered more hope. It even had an advert from a language school. Lucy had been prepared by her tutor to expect nothing from languages except voluntary work abroad so this advert was a nice surprise; but something in her was frightened to find out that she wasn't good enough, that her degree and A levels didn't really amount to anything. In fact, Lucy was in favour of becoming good at something else before she put her languages to use. Her gut told her that she would apply herself better, take more risks and act outside the box, if she wasn't completely dependent on her learned skills, her badge. She cut out the advert after checking what was on the back of it, and put it aside.

More skilled trades, care, chef and work from home opportunities filled the rest of three pages. There was a selection of sales positions, selling telecoms, gas, electricity and dietary supplements but most were commission based and if she hadn't had the language school option set aside, she might have allowed herself to feel depressed.

Buenos Spanish School wanted a sales person to sell their new English language course to Europeans in Spain, Poland, Germany and Italy. Apparently these countries had grants available so no money was required but Lucy would be working on her own, supervised directly by the managing director, selling a course that didn't yet exist.

So, in comparison, unfortunately, her original offer now looked like the best she would get. It looked as though Lucy would be a sales adviser on Monday.

AUTHOR'S NOTE

Lucy has no option other than to go with the flow and she is dismayed to be scraping the barrel and lowering her social valuation. Fortunately, she recognises working in sales as a lateral career move that will add direction and purpose to her language skills, so the long term benefit outweighs the short term cost.

All that would
come out was

"eek!"

– but it spurred
her on.

5. Fear

Now Lucy was prepared to have fun. It was Saturday and two days off the drink had done her the world of good. She was making a pot of coffee for herself and her friend Natalie who was popping in before they spent a day at the shops, then lunch and the cinema too, if anything good was on. Natalie was fun, especially considering she had been studying for her law degree. Her friends were all very square but Natalie didn't mind making a fool of herself, which always made Lucy feel less self conscious. In a small way, they were celebrities, as they had camped for tickets at Wimbledon for the past five years. They always wore outrageous outfits that had relevance to the latest British hopeful so the papers loved them. Her high social media profile was one of the reasons the recruitment agent had offered Lucy the job.

The lawyers had organised only two after exam events so Natalie had plenty of spare cash and Lucy had a little, because she had budgeted for the two days of drinking that she had missed.

Pauline and her new boyfriend were snoring loudly in her room and a strange man in fluorescent clothing was out for the count on the sofa.

Natalie was always late so Lucy took her time and her coffee to have a look at the details of her job offer. It was simply a list of facts about an impressive company called Bestcell, based in Poole, not far from her dad's house. Lucy would be part of a team selling business intelligence software, whatever that was. She was told to start at nine in the morning, finish at half past five in the afternoon with an hour for lunch. A basic salary plus a generous commission was on offer. A footnote reminded her to take her national insurance number and tax code if she had one.

Her trusty Nissan Micra would get her there. Lucy called her Ellie. Ellie had only broken down once but Lucy had only owned her for a month when that happened and it frightened her. Ellie had really broken down and needed the AA to transport her to a local garage, who wanted to charge a fortune for the repair. Fortunately, her mum and dad had extracted Ellie from the garage and redelivered her to a local man who loved Micras, and had several in various states of dismantle in his garden. He fixed Ellie for next to nothing and pledged to help again every time she needed it. In a funny way, it was a shame they hadn't needed him since.

Natalie arrived in a swirl of perfume, scarves and shopping bags. She had several things to return and was full of the joys of the world. Exams were over and she, like most of the student lawyers, had secured some sort of relevant post. Natalie was a court runner but she knew she would get on quickly and Lucy was jealous of her because, knowing Natalie, she would enjoy herself too.

'So, tell!" demanded Natalie. "What horrors have you agreed to?" They kept each other up to date by texts, Facebook and Twitter but Lucy repeated the story while Natalie sipped her coffee, making concerned sounds as she thought fit. When Lucy had finished, Natalie announced, "I am so jealous. Sales is a mystery. There are no rules and there is everything to gain because you start with nothing, whereas the law is a pre-agreed process and all I have to do is fit into someone else's shoes." Lucy hadn't seen it like that and was pleased. She was also surprised to hear that Natalie might be jealous of her. "And it pays the bills!" they chanted together, clinking coffee cups.

The chap in fluorescent clothing stumbled past them, mumbling something about a good morning and he fiddled with the door latch until it ejected him onto the street and into the daylight. Both girls gave each other a look that said "rather him than me."

Shopping was an orgy of excited contact, comparison and conclusions. Natalie returned all her items but they didn't buy a lot except an essential work suit each. Natalie chose regulation solicitor black but Lucy choose burgundy and black court shoes with slender heels that, she thought, made her legs long, elegant and grown up.

Lunch was simple, as always. Salad and garlic bread for Lucy and a Margherita for Natalie. They shared a bottle of chilled white wine and a lot of stories from the past five years which put them in the mood for a good movie by mid afternoon.

Jack was recruited to join them and a group of Natalie's friends that evening but Lucy had to negotiate a very grumpy Pauline on her return. She didn't say anything but her crashing around said it all. Lucy didn't care, she was glad to have avoided more senseless spending and drinking. She had a job and the clothes and money for a lovely night out with Jack and her best friend.

Monday was a beautiful day and the sun dazzled her into a state of alert. She couldn't eat but forced down half a cup of tea. She was to meet Martin, her manager, at what looked more like a residential address, which was strange.

The door was definitely that of someone's home. A lady holding a baby answered. "Hello," said Lucy. "Is Martin Hopkins available please?" "You must be Lucy," said the lady. "I'm Corrine and this little person is Egalin. Martin is somewhere. Martin!" she shouted behind her. "Come and look after this beautiful young lady," chastised Corrine as he clumped along the hall. "Hi," he said. "My name is Martin and this is my wife." "Yes, thank you," cut in Corrine. "We have done all that." "Okay." he said, "This is our home but I have an office in the garden." "Phew, that makes sense I suppose," thought Lucy.

Martin led the way along a covered passageway that was strewn with decorating equipment and baby paraphernalia. "Excuse all this," said Martin. "We are decorating the baby's room and we are a bit short on space." He had a worldly look about him, a face that would be shocked by anything while accepting of everything at the same time. Lucy felt safe and that was always her number one priority.

The office was a summer house that must have been chosen from the 'tiny summer houses section' of any garden centre. He had obviously taken a lot of care to board it out on the inside to reduce damp, increase warmth and hide cabling but there was only one computer, one phone and one chair. Lucy stared at it, not really recognising it as the premises which were fated to launch her career. "Oh, I will go and get you a chair," said Martin. "Would you like a cup of coffee?." He returned with two coffees slopping over the top and a heavy garden chair. Once settled, he asked: "So, what's your plan?" If anyone had thought 'gulp', it was Lucy right then! She, of course, didn't have a clue. She had only finished her finals nine days ago and now here she was on a garden chair, in a garden shed, sipping strong coffee and advising a grown businessman on his sales. The first thing that popped into her mind was that she needed the money and the next, reassuringly, was that the recruiter had been convinced she could do the job. So, very naturally, she said: "To contact your customers and find out what they want to hear from you." Lucy waited for an explosion of dissatisfaction but instead, was delighted to hear Martin launch into a three hour long history of business intelligence and his company. "Could it be that easy?" she allowed herself to think.

It turned out that the company did employ a sales force but it mainly comprised franchisees like Martin who didn't know anything about selling. At least he had been wise enough to employ some expertise but "the poor chap has ended up with me," thought Lucy. It was already lunchtime and Corrine had fixed them an exotic salad and rye bread. She was from Israel and Lucy learned that they had lived in New Zealand for the past seven years but wanted to raise Egalin in England.

They were a lovely couple, so welcoming and friendly and Lucy hoped she would be able to meet their expectations. A client meeting was booked for three o'clock that afternoon and Lucy fully expected to tag along but it turned out that Martin expected her to stay and make some calls. "Who will I be calling?" she ventured. "Oh, I have a database of companies with a turnover in excess of ten million pounds per annum. I don't know if the names are any good but these companies are an exact match for what we have to offer," explained Martin.

Lucy had picked up the implications of 'turnover' and 'exact match' from the morning but it took a second longer for her to realise that Martin expected her to call these companies. To cold call these companies – on her own.

"OMG," she thought, I am totally unqualified to do this but all she could do was to reply "Okay" and Martin sorted out the list on his computer, explaining that the office telephone was simply an extension of the house phone. Lucy was sweating down her back and her silk shirt was sticking to her, inside her new jacket. She hoped she didn't smell. At least she wouldn't have to walk too much in her new shoes she thought, and smiled at him. "I'll be back before you go." he said. "Good luck!" And off he went.

She Googled 'selling business intelligence' and was offered a list of competitors and job offers like hers. Interestingly, none were with the same organisation but she found an article on Wikipedia entitled 'collaborative selling'. It seemed that serving the customers' customer was the aim but who were Martin's customers' customers'? "Damn." She should have asked him. But wouldn't he have mentioned this if he knew? And he hadn't. "Interesting," thought Lucy. "I don't think he or his organisation has a clue." She smiled. "At least I can't go too far wrong."

The first company on Martin's list was a name Lucy knew. She recognised it as one that owned a number of the shops she frequented. The named decision maker was the Managing Director so she called and asked for him. "Wasn't that how it worked?" she questioned silently. "Who is calling?" asked the receptionist. Lucy told the lady her name. "Where are you from?" persisted the lady. Lucy said the full name of her new employer hoping that would do it, but, no. "And what is the call about?" asked the woman, critically. Lucy could hardly bear it. Why was this person being so mean? She didn't know what to say. She hadn't been trained. How could she know? She hated Martin, she hated the recruiter and she realised she was going to burst into tears in a second; so she forced herself to reply: "Oh, don't worry. I'll try again later." She put down the receiver and immediately burst into a flood of tears, real, wet tears, accompanied by an instance of chest-clenching anguish that represented all the bottled up emotion from the past six months. Exam worries, money worries and fear of the future. It was all too much and she cried noisily until Corrine knocked politely on the door with a concerned look on her face. Lucy told her the whole story and Corrine was convinced that Martin was going to be understanding.

Unfortunately, Lucy knew she couldn't continue to work with the memories of that failed call.

How could sales be so hard? Why did she feel so small, after having only spoken to one receptionist? She hadn't planned to bully or persist. All she had wanted to do was to try and connect with another human being and it hadn't worked.

AUTHOR'S NOTE

Lucy is in awe of the responsibility presented by an outbound cold sales call and is shocked by the enormous amount of psychology packed into the first sixty seconds. By just doing it, she puts herself in a stressful situation and her adrenalin pulls her through but she learns at an enhanced rate. Lucy is careful to maximise her chances of an enjoyable and profitable future by compartmentalising what she has learned.

Doing nothing is not an option

"Yewgh!"

She couldn't help
screwing up her face
as she pulled away,
deciding to do
it herself.

6. Disgust

Her dad was out. In fact, she remembered, he may have gone up North to do a talk for the CCA. Jack was abroad trying out his new life with the ocean and the only friends she had nearby were Jack's student friends who had probably all gone elsewhere now. She would just have to work out what to do on her own.

Lucy gave her predicament some thought. She needed the money, that was fact one and Martin would probably let her continue, fact two; but in her heart, she knew that these facts had to be ignored. Her dad had always said: "If you have only one skill and that skill is to be comfortable with change, you will need nothing else."

She was sure her decision to quit after only one day would not be popular with Lynne but she had learned to trust that most people will do their best to make good of a bad situation and she couldn't do anything about replacing herself in a new town and a profession that was new to her; so she chose one of her dad's many foreign films, cooked some pasta and settled in with a glass of wine and a blanket.

She woke early and lay still, thinking. Lynne wouldn't be in until eight thirty so she had time for a shower, breakfast and a look at her emails.

Lynne answered on the first ring and was disappointed that Lucy didn't want to continue but understood, admitting that they were having trouble recruiting for Bestcell. "It's clear that the franchisees should get themselves some sales training," she said and asked: "Are you free today?" "Why?" asked Lucy. "Because, I have another position for you with much more support from a female boss. It's in town, in an office, and you could start after lunch today, at two this afternoon."

Lucy couldn't believe that sales jobs were so easy to get. How could someone, completely unqualified like herself, be offered two positions in a row like this? she wondered. Surely there were hundreds of others keen to work in sales? Lucy's silence prompted

Lynne to say: "The salary is more but there is no commission."
"Okay, great. Thank you," replied Lucy, and took the details.

This was the same position that she had seen in the paper, the same language school, looking for someone to sell a new course. "Oh well," thought Lucy, "I am closer to success than yesterday."

Had she left Martin any closer to a sale? Not actually, but she was sure that explaining it all to her would have helped him work it out better in his own mind. She called to apologise and was surprised to hear him apologising to her for putting her in an awkward position and promising to pay her via the agency, which was a great relief.

She washed her dishes and switched on the radio. Her dad often listened to Radio 4 and a Rabbi was talking about the war in Afghanistan, concluding in a way that was very relevant to Lucy by saying: "Remember, your enemies will not listen to what you say."

Maybe she had considered that receptionist to be an enemy or maybe she in turn had seen Lucy as an enemy, trying to steal her boss's time. How could she know? Perhaps Lucy sounded like an enemy.

Ester welcomed Lucy with warm, open Spanish arms. She was delighted to have some help with the selling. She had done nothing about it except decide that they had something to sell. Lucy chatted with her freely in Spanish while they drank cappuccino from packets, which was disgusting. Ester wanted Lucy to sell places on an English language course to students from Spain, Germany, Poland and Italy. She had no idea how to do it but thought that it should be a profitable venture. Lucy was delighted to be given free reign but couldn't help feel the pressure of being a standalone profit centre. It sounded like her employment depended completely on her own success. "Well, at least I can combine telephone sales with my languages," she thought.

The first port of call was the language agents in Spain. These small companies attracted groups and individuals to go and learn

English in England so the call was immediately collaborative, with Lucy and the agent working out how to serve their customers together. Lucy smiled and took a deep breath to make her voice sound calm and relaxed in an effort to sound friendly and concerned. The approach was clearly working, most agents were happy to speak to her and she actually started to enjoy herself.

The difficulty seemed to be that several language schools already offered courses in Bournemouth and some had good and long-standing reputations; but even the agents who had agreements with these established schools were interested to hear about an exciting new idea.

There was a part of Lucy that really admired Patty and Selma in the Simpsons and their devotion to McGuyver. It had been interesting to study them watching him extract himself from predicaments, like being tied to a chair in the locked room of a burning building. Their tutor had paused the DVD at that point and they had all tried to guess what feats he would attempt to achieve his goal. They rarely came anywhere close but got better at guessing as they watched more episodes. This was not so much because they learned his pattern of behaviour but because they found that their own creativity improved. One of the boys, who had a rich and successful father in business, said that his dad said: "Anyone can do a job but to be really good at it, you have to be creative." Lucy had really embraced this concept and was pleased to be able to put her creativity to the test.

On her second call she had a really long conversation with an agent in Poland. Kriss had worked at a larger agency but had recently started his own company and was very interested in building a relationship with a language school in England. He explained that to compete with the larger schools and agencies they had to offer better rates of success.

Lucy ascertained that there was a standard number of hours studying per week and then students were pretty much left to their own devices after class.

At university, Lucy had always enjoyed the buddying system which demanded that they choose someone in their tutor group who they would only converse with in Spanish. At first they had avoided each other but as one pair started to get into it, the others were obliged to compete and towards the end of the course, buddies had adopted a Spanish persona and therefore learned at the fastest possible rate, even thinking and sometimes dreaming in Spanish.

Lucy immediately identified that Kriss's customers would benefit from buddying with the English students who were learning Spanish at the school, and her genius was that their English students would get a free benefit and would probably enjoy sharing the New Forest, beaches and night life in Bournemouth. The conclusion of the conversation was that Kriss would visit once Lucy had confirmed the conversation by email and she was ecstatic with her very real result.

Ester felt differently. "How big is the company?" she asked. Lucy explained and found herself persuading Ester to see the opportunity as a good one. They agreed to send the email but Lucy found that they didn't have the experience, marketing material or even words to support what she had been charged with selling.

She now doubted herself but decided to make more calls to increase her evidence. When she now raised the concept of their buddying system, everyone was willing to tell her about what they were doing; and by the end of her first day she had found an established agency willing to visit when they were next in Bournemouth, several happy to add them to their list of suppliers and of course, Kriss. So although Ester still hadn't complimented her, Lucy went home very pleased with herself because she felt that she had really connected with a number of human beings who had a common requirement.

They spent half of the next day working on the email and Lucy made some calls to the agents that she hadn't been able to contact the day before, adding three more to the list of potential customers. Ester grumbled that the best leads were either too small or too large and that the rest were just being polite.

Lucy was hurt because she had felt that she had done a good job. Consequently she struggled to maintain her enthusiasm when Ester asked her to call German and Italian agents. She knew enough to say hello and ask for the boss and after that, they were all reasonably happy to speak English; so she enjoyed many more involved conversations but Lucy couldn't quite bring herself to invite anyone to visit now, so she simply agreed for her employer to be considered as a future supplier.

Ester seemed happier to have nothing to do and she seemed petrified to find out that her school wasn't good enough. It was almost as though she wanted an excuse to simply continue teaching Spanish to English students. Lucy was worried because she had called all the agents on the list and only had a handful to try again.

Early next morning, Lynne called Lucy's mobile to say that Ester didn't need her any more. Lucy was gutted but only in a way, because she wasn't comfortable working for a boss who didn't seem to have an open mind.

AUTHOR'S NOTE

Lucy has been careful to identify that no-one knows any better. Although she would readily accept any advice, she is equally happy to be free to find out for herself. Now she can experiment and make mistakes without looking bad which means that she will be learning faster and more thoroughly from her own experience.

“Oh, yeah!”

describes the look on her face. A job well done or a big deal, but you can fake it too.

7. Satisfaction

“Ha,” thought Lucy. “I’m free, and I’m going to be a good sales adviser. It’s sunny and my dad has left his ‘run around’ for me.” She dressed for shopping with no money and sent a text to what was Jack’s Bournemouth group of friends. The growl of the 2.3 litre engine came as a pleasant surprise and she smiled because it felt good to have all this power at her command.

She was a good driver and her dad had made a point that she should use the Mercedes whenever it suited her. With a scarf to hold her long blonde hair in place and sun glasses, she looked stunning as the car grumbled along the sea front into Bournemouth.

She parked centrally and saw that Melissa was free for coffee at noon.

Lucy enjoyed the attention of the bored male shop assistants and, just to please them, wiggled slightly more than she needed to in her tight skirt.

Melissa was working in a trendy bar until late and envied Lucy’s determination to make a break from the easy repetition of catering work. They killed a few hours and looked beautiful together but envied everyone else for their purpose, drive and money.

They kissed and hugged goodbye as Lucy took a call from Lynne. She was to start an inbound telephone sales role for a company selling promotional products and she was to report to Max at nine in the morning the next day. Apparently the company was an easy walk from her dad’s house so she took a peek on her way home. It looked good and she felt good.

Lucy had travelled a lot for a twenty three year old. Divorced parents meant two holidays a year and her dad’s windsurfing adventures took her to very different places to her mum’s horse riding holidays; plus, she had made a point of travelling to France and Spain, working where possible in all her holidays.

Her new manager, Max, seemed like a genuinely good man. He was only a little older than Lucy and had clearly done well for himself, working in his dad's company. There were genuine smiles all round in the small-scale open-plan environment in which Lucy was to join three others taking inbound sales calls.

She liked Andy. Although he seemed a little older, he had a knowing smile and a cute look from under his hair when he thought he may have pushed a joke too far. Karen was most friendly but Lucy couldn't help mark her as a rival, being blonde and well proportioned too. Charlotte was an odd one, very careful with her personality; but Lucy could tell she would be a good friend if you could get close enough.

Lucy had a week of training which essentially meant learning the rules and tools. They seemed to have access to an unlimited number of promotional products and Lucy was very impressed with the computer system, although the number of screens and procedures did seem daunting. "Well, at least I should last a little longer here," she mused as she watched Lindsay in customer services process one of Max's sales. Lucy worried about the repetition of these procedures; she knew that she preferred options.

Max kept calling her over and pointing at his headset while he was on the phone. Lucy took this to mean that she should listen and she had to admire his energy, enthusiasm and direction. He was always moving towards the next deal and rarely spoke of what he had come away from. That seemed to be Lindsay's job. He showed a lot of interest in Lucy, what she had done in her life to date and her relationship with selling, and Lucy told the whole truth because she sensed that any embellishment would soon be exposed.

She was surprised to find out that she would be considered an optimist, finding an opportunity in every difficulty, but she was what Max called 'external' – needing the approval of others before she knew something had been done well. He said that this was just the right profile for a telephone sales adviser but as they talked, Lucy began to get the feeling that he was very self-orientated.

When he talked about football he described himself as a striker but seemed to rarely play in that position and yet in every match, all goals seemed to have been set up by him. He was clearly one hundred per cent driven by the next deal and he was only really interested in what was immediately valuable to him; but Lucy considered that there was a time to be self-orientated and a time to be others-orientated.

AUTHOR'S NOTE

So much is new to Lucy these days. She is testing her understanding of everything, challenging her own behaviour and absorbing information from everyone around her. As a consequence, she is learning what and who to trust but she needs to be careful to take time to have fun and nurture her own sense of self.

“Ooer.”

Sadness is a common emotion but useful and usually only temporary.

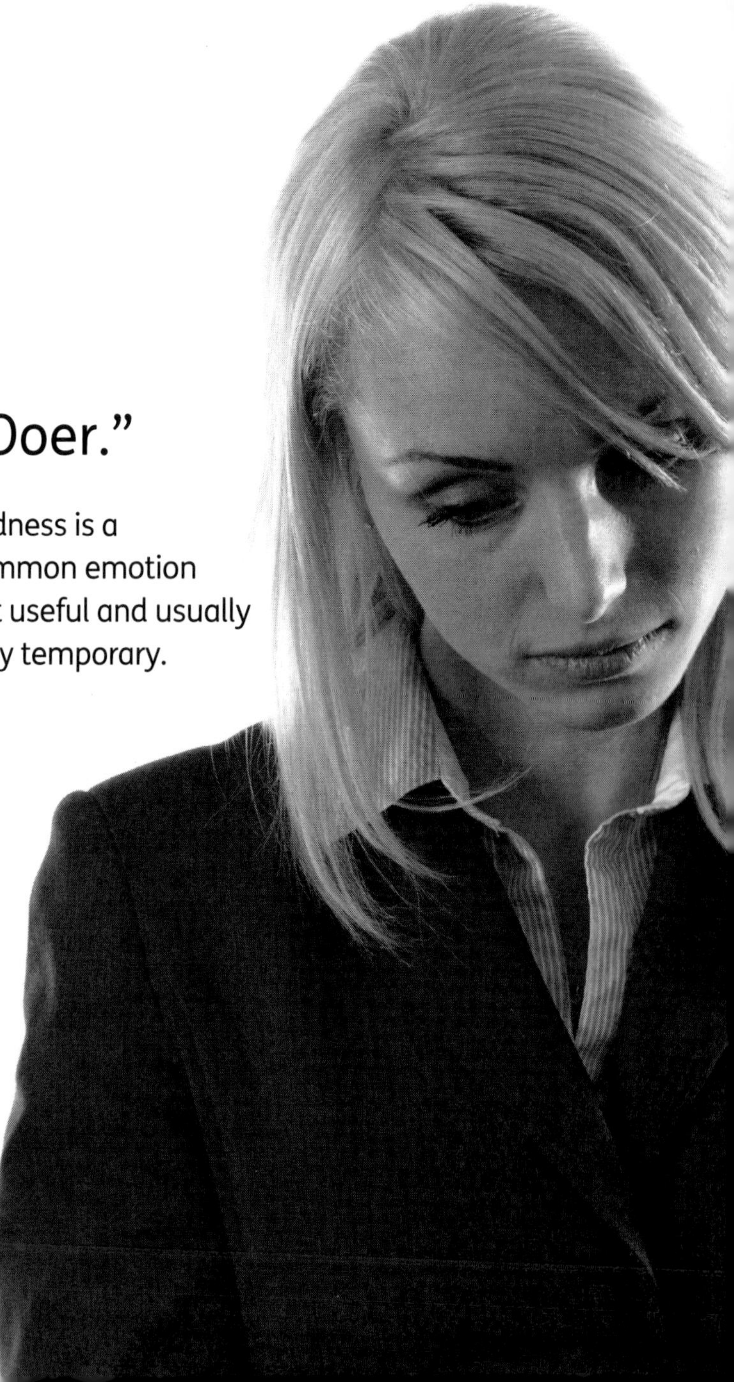

8. Sadness

Monday was a frightening prospect because Lucy was going on the dialler which meant that she was going to receive incoming calls and most callers would be interested in a quotation for one or more promotional items. Lucy wasn't afraid to speak to them – after all, they were only people; but she was a little afraid of all the screens that needed her attention during the call.

Max had reassured her that he would be on hand to help with any problems but Lucy didn't want her social valuation to slip in comparison to the incoming caller. "No, that wasn't it. I don't want to look bad in front of my colleagues," she thought. Sure, she was new and had a lot to learn but she couldn't help recognise that everything she did was being valued by the room, especially the girls.

She had dressed sombrely because she wanted to keep a low profile at first so as to optimise her chances of looking better as each day went by. Thinking about it, Lucy was surprised to recognise how afraid she was of making a mistake, doing wrong and looking bad. "What is wrong with me?" she thought. Making mistakes is learning. Hadn't her dad always said "if you're not falling off, you're not trying hard enough." Her phone rang. "Oh, why do I have to be the first to take a call on a Monday?" she thought, and was acutely aware that everyone was listening to her.

The caller sounded friendly enough so it was easy to sound relaxed. Carl ran his own product design company in Leicester and employed three designers who were attending a trade show later in the year. Their customers were twenty five to fifty five years old, operation managers and mainly men who were responsible for managing their product portfolio efficiently.

Lucy found all this out during a comfortable chat. Carl wanted one thousand mechanical pencils that would take their logo and Lucy suggested that he also consider executive folders and mugs, which she thought would be attractive to his customers. She could give him prices on the pencils and mugs immediately but Max was busy on a call, so Lucy promised to call him back soon with a price for the folders.

"And relax," she told herself as she put the phone down. She shot a glance around the room. Max was pounding his potential customer with reasons to buy, Karen was talking sweetly, too sweetly, to someone about USB sticks and Charlotte was having a lot of fun telling a potential supplier of delivery services that she would transfer him to their 'purchaser', who didn't exist. Charlotte put the phone down with a satisfied smile on her face, took a moment, looked at Lucy and said: "If they want pencils, sell them pencils." Lucy blushed. She had been very pleased with herself for tripling a six hundred pound enquiry.

Charlotte's phone rang and Lucy waited for Max, who was very pleased that she was getting on and coached her through the various procedures, to send a quotation by email. After a few more calls, Lucy still had a strong sense of unease; but while she was getting a cup of coffee from the machine, Andy came up to her and asked: "Can I have a word?" By the tone of his voice, Lucy assumed she had done him wrong, but was in the mood to receive all useful opinions. Andy, however, went on to ask: "How do you do that?" "Do what?" asked Lucy. "Speak to the customers like you do – be so familiar with them?"

Lucy had enjoyed reading "How to win friends and influence people" by Dale Carnegie many years ago but had found the old fashioned references quite frustrating, which meant that the only lesson she had taken away was to think and act like an enthusiastic, well-meaning and compliant dog. Andy clearly liked what he heard and she could hear him trying to adopt this approach for the rest of the day; but to Lucy's ear, he was struggling. She had heard a little about his recent break-up from his long-term girlfriend, loss of the flat and his television and stereo. She assumed he must be in a difficult place and that was what she could hear in his voice.

Being the youngest by far of several children in her family had naturally put Lucy in an acquisitive state of mind. She assumed that people knew more than she did and was always determined to extract everything that they knew, assuming it would add to her own valuation. Once she had extracted their map of the world, there was usually an obvious collaboration, or at least enough learning, to have justified her effort. It was interesting to think that her sound might have a relationship with her experience.

Andy asked her if she wanted to go for a drink after work and Lucy was tempted. She liked Andy but she had promised herself to replace drink and the pub as a focus for her social life so she asked him if he wanted to come for a swim instead. “Oh, I don’t have my trunks or a towel,” he laughed but Lucy persisted, she didn’t want him to give up so easily. She was interested to know how much he wanted a date with her so she said: “You can borrow a pair of my dad’s trunks and a towel of course. You are about the same size.”

“Which pool do you have in mind?” he asked, looking a little worried; but Lucy could see him battling with himself. “Not a pool, we are going to swim in the sea.” “In the sea, what, in England?” he exclaimed. “Of course in the sea, it will be about eighteen degrees centigrade thanks to the hot May and June you have had here.” Lucy was partly driven by the fact that she didn’t know anyone in Christchurch and she didn’t really want to spend another evening on her own. They worked out the details and walked to her dad’s house, through the woods.

The beach was busy and Andy looked really self-conscious but Lucy respected him a lot for pushing his boundaries. The sea felt cold because it was a hot day but their bodies soon adapted and they swam out to the four hundred yard buoy, which is where boats have to slow down to four miles an hour. Lucy was a strong swimmer and she pointed out the far buoy to him. She planned to swim there one day. The distance wouldn’t be a problem but being so exposed, being so far out, might be. She hoped to conquer that fear one day. Andy didn’t seem at all keen to stay chatting out there and Lucy completely understood; so they swam back, lay in the sun until it cooled and went back to her dad’s house. She offered him dinner but he voiced his concern about getting home. “Oh, come on!” was all it took to persuade him. They ate pasta, peas, tuna and cheese all, mixed up. It was one of Lucy's specialities and, with a bottle of chilled white wine on the balcony overlooking the beach, it seemed to be the perfect complement to their sea swim.

He looked like a different person out of work. Maybe it was the wine or the smell of expensive shower gel or even the clothes she had insisted he borrow from her dad's casual collection, but Lucy really wanted him. She knew her relationship with Jack couldn't last and he knew it, too. They had discussed it and agreed that if they still wanted to be together when he came home, they would give it a go; but neither were holding their breath.

Andy needed very little persuasion and Lucy found him to be a decisive, adventurous and considerate lover. They hardly slept at all that night and enjoyed their morning coffee on the balcony, watching the mist lift off the sea. Lucy quizzed him about work and he was as helpful as he could be; but although he had been selling for ten years, he really couldn't say what it was that actually triggered a sale.

They returned to work separately and were easily logged onto the system by nine. Lucy's fatigue was overcome by euphoria but she could see that Andy was suffering. It was clear that Charlotte had sussed them out and was making comments that threatened to expose them. Lucy didn't care. What they had done was only natural and if the bosses took a dim view of it, well, Lucy considered that to be a representation of the superficial approach to sales that she was beginning to recognise. If only Charlotte put as much energy into getting to know her customers, she would be a brilliant sales adviser.

The day wore on and Lucy could hear Max closing, closing and closing. It was an effective technique but Lucy couldn't help think that if she were a customer, she would find it rather annoying. She wondered how many customers regretted their decision soon after and imagined if they did, they would probably cost the customer services team a lot of time. Karen was like a photographic negative of Max. She flirted mercilessly with men and women and Lucy considered she would enjoy being on the other end of attention like that; but Karen often forgot to ask for the order, using instead phrases like: "Are you sort of ready to make a decision?" And Andy, although he had served her well, still sounded 'wrong' on the phone. She knew that he meant well but his many issues were clearly represented by the sound of his voice.

It seemed that Friday nights were a 'big thing' to Lucy's new colleagues and they invited her along with a passion which seemed misplaced. Friday was a 'casual dress day' and as soon as they met their sales target for the week, the radio would be switched on. Fortunately, it was never early enough for the Chris Moyles Show. Lucy had always had a problem with group culture and she couldn't help feeling that the tone of his early morning show was a clarion call to all those who couldn't be bothered to think about their own behaviour, attend gigs and make reference to artists, sessions and refer to music festivals as something 'to be done'.

She respected that it was hard to recognise that you didn't actually have to go, that it was possible to retain independent thought, and this brought her back to her own dilemma. Was she going to join the big Friday drinking session or not? She had chosen a pretty summer dress and gladiator sandals and felt good, too good to present herself as a victim to the pubs and bars hoping to sell her the impossible dream. She said "yes" but really had no intention of going along.

Fortunately, her deception was unnecessary, although the circumstances were far from ideal. Max passed her on his way out of his dad's office at ten to five, when she had been summoned to attend, and Lucy noted his cold shoulder. Albert struggled to smile at the best of times but at this moment he was all business and said: "Right, Lucy, I won't beat about the bush. Your contract clearly forbids you to have a relationship with a colleague and I have heard that you have broken this rule. Is that true?" Lucy wasn't going to beat around the bush either and she wasn't going to allow the fear of loss to interfere with her own sense of self so she replied: "Yes," looking Albert straight in the eye.

They let her go but paid her immediately so she actually felt quite well off for the first time in many years, partly because her account was heading towards the black and partly because she had really got her teeth into something new. She had closed her first sale that day and had literally asked herself out loud: "I wonder if there is a formula for selling?"

AUTHOR'S NOTE

Lucy is beginning to recognise that how she sounds when she talks really matters. By listening to Andy, she is starting to realise that her sound might change with circumstances, and she is beginning to appreciate that she can manipulate the sound to improve her chances of success on the phone.

It hardly matters what you say, it's how you say it that makes the difference

It is so easy to know when someone is happy – but great to have it confirmed.

"Woohoo!"

9. Joy

Lucy was fairly sure that everything she had read about selling was wrong. She had a gut feeling that getting on the customer's side and finding out what they liked about the product and/or service before coming to terms was the route to enjoyable, profitable, and – most importantly for her – sustainable sales. She had the whole weekend ahead of her, money in the bank and a house to herself, because her dad wouldn't be back until Sunday evening.

Lucy texted Melissa and gave the house a thorough cleaning in her underwear with the surround house music system turned right up. She hoped the neighbours would tolerate it for a while.

The freedom of movement, oxygenated blood and sense of achievement helped her reach a state of excitement and she laughed out loud when Melissa invited Lucy to join her to chaperone a band around town for the evening before their performance.

Melissa looked voluptuous with her brunette hair cascading down her back and her friend Gaytree looked like an Asian doll; so when blonde Lucy made the trio they looked like a perfect set of Barbie dolls. The band was clearly pleased with this association and they played their part with quick-witted and cynical conversation, focussing on how good they thought their band was; but the girls were on expenses and therefore on great form, giving the boys a good run for their money. Bournemouth, being the great place it is to party, meant that the time flew by and Lucy was surprised when Melissa announced that they had to take the boys to prepare for their performance.

Three pretty females looked startlingly out of place in the demonic environment of a basement club and without the boys' attention they felt a little uneasy; but, they applied themselves wholeheartedly to the pulsating noise, simple dance, rough and tumble.

The boys were on a high after a great performance. It was late but none of the six were in a mood to end the night so Lucy didn't have to persuade them too hard to take a taxi back to Christchurch, where she gathered all they needed for a night on the beach.

A small fire and candles buried in the sand created a wonderfully bohemian atmosphere and the girls sang along to Mark's heroic attempt at playing her dad's old guitar. A lot of kissing went on but the two groups were very respectful of each other and the girls retired to their tent with satisfaction in their hearts.

The boys were from Manchester and were astounded to wake among the sand dunes by a sunny sea. They packed up and strolled along to the beach cafe for breakfast. They all needed several hours more sleep or caffeine, which came with their breakfast; so they chatted long into the morning. It was clear that Mark, who was the lead guitarist and singer, fancied Lucy, but Lucy wasn't so sure. He was good looking, clean-cut and polite, but that was a thin veneer over a volcanic aggression that was hidden only by razor-sharp cynicism. He kept Ronnie and Lou in place with this social tool and they didn't seem to notice; but if they stood out of line he would draw a cartoon of the miscreant, putting them at the centre of the group's ghoulish attention. Ronnie and Gaytree were holding hands under the table and Melissa clearly had the hots for Lou, but he didn't seem bothered.

Lucy considered inviting them all back to lounge around the pool but she could see that might get out of hand and she didn't want to worry about the mess or cause her dad any problems. Plus, she wanted to focus on her next career move; so she invited them all to share a taxi back to Bournemouth, a journey she knew she wouldn't take.

On the journey home the five considered it strange that Lucy would choose to spend a weekend by herself. Lucy, however, was delighted to be on her own. She enjoyed her own company during the day and was even more pleased with herself now that she had topped off a good week with a great Friday night; but she needed to sleep so she lay by the pool in the shade of a tree and listened to the afternoon play. It was an interesting story about a peasant girl in nineteenth century Paris who was slowly improving her lot. Lucy could relate to the heroine but couldn't help nodding off.

She woke with a start, chilled now that the sun had withdrawn its warmth from the shade. She staggered to her feet, shivered and dived into the pool. She knew the exercise would wake her up and warm her blood and thirty lengths were enough to put her in a positive frame of mind. After a hot shower, she put on her jogging pants and hoodie, baked a potato and tended to her Facebook account. Three hours later she was tired but wired so she poured herself a glass of wine and watched a few episodes of House MD on DVD.

The seagulls woke her early on Sunday. She had slept well but had a cold arm so she nursed it under the duvet while she planned her day. On the face of it, she had nothing to do but she had learned that there was always plenty to do. The morning was overcast so she scheduled indoor tasks first because it was predicted to be sunny later. She wanted more exercise so she planned a sea swim before lunch and she wanted to keep her languages up to date so her novel was pencilled in for the afternoon. She could always watch a movie later while waiting for her dad to return. She looked forward to seeing him again, very much.

Lucy knew this state of being half asleep and half awake in the morning was known by hypnotherapists as hypnopompia and she had learned that it was the ideal time to think; so she dozed on and asked herself: "What is the right thing to do about my job?"

It was clear that she should apply to an organisation that depended on outbound sales calls. Even to her innocent eyes the banks were selling all the time, and she presumed that outbound calls were the reason for their phenomenal success. Her plan to swim, read her book and watch a movie all fell into place after that so Lucy got up, had one cup of tea to get her going and dedicated the rest of the day to doing without it. She often restricted herself like this on a Sunday, and sometimes over the whole weekend, but knew she was in for a 'lack of caffeine' headache by lunchtime.

The benefit was how very enlivening coffee throughout the week would be, even after this short time off.

Her CV didn't need a lot of tweaking for the banks and there were several in Bournemouth so she attached or pasted it into emails where applicable and by lunchtime, she had the results of seven applications to look forward to.

Her dad looked shattered when he came in. "Hello, sweetie," he said warmly, while giving her a lovely deep hug and a kiss on the cheek. She relaxed because this was her safest place in the world. "I am going for a run," he announced. "I've been sitting down for days, eating and drinking way too much tea and coffee." Lucy offered to cook his favourite meal and he gave her a big grin. "That would be lovely," he said, "and you can tell me how you are getting on."

Lucy explained it all and her dad listened actively. "You are doing exactly the right thing," he said. "Starting at the bottom, learning from everyone and being willing to make mistakes. Customers are the same as bosses who are the same as friends. They all start wanting some, then they want more and when they have that, they want it more efficiently. It is only then, when they are safe and secure, that they consider sharing it, but only as a means to identify what's next. You are brilliant with people so you are going to be brilliant with customers my darling. You will get a call first thing tomorrow, I am sure of it. Do you fancy a game of chess?"

AUTHOR'S NOTE

Since the age of seventeen, Lucy has lived her life like a storybook which ensures that she has a constant stream of goals and targets to meet. The obvious benefit of this approach to life is that she finds it easy to know when to congratulate herself in preparation for the next step.

Life is just a series of changes

Hissing

“Yesss,”

with a sharp
nod of her head,
clearly indicates
the excitement
she feels.

10. Excitement

Lucy did get a call soon after nine on Monday, just as her dad had predicted. It was from one of the building societies in Bournemouth who were looking for telephone-based insurance advisers. They were a big name so Lucy was flattered and the salary was one which would allow her to be independent, get her own flat and plan for the future. She was excited and a little frightened but they were impressed with her application and told her so. The interview was that afternoon and she was enrolled to their training programme at nine the following day because someone had dropped out at the last minute.

Lucy didn't want to stand out or draw attention to herself so she dressed in nicely cut grey trousers, a pretty cotton top and a cardigan because it was chilly in the mornings now. She knew she would work out the bus timetable soon but for now she would drive in because there were several all-day car parks available for only four pounds a day. She drove herself along the sea front to cheer herself up before a whole day trapped indoors and she wondered if cycling to work was a possibility. Her diet and exercise regime were responsible for her very clear skin and she was proud to be one of those girls who only wore makeup on special occasions; but her lack of preening only contributed to her being extra early on her first day, an hour ahead of schedule.

She could tell that the trainer, who bustled in at eight thirty, was impressed but a little annoyed. Lucy was sitting calmly at her hutch with a machine coffee, chatting to two boys. Her new colleagues had worked in sales since school and had some fantastic stories. She felt a little in awe of them but somehow superior at the same time. Lucy wondered how she would compare. In one way, they were successful sales advisers already, having earned their living from selling for four years but in another way they had failed at what they had been doing and were starting again, here.

She wondered why this valuation was so important to her. What was she afraid of? Perhaps potential customers had the same feelings when they received a sales call from a company who were essentially saying that they knew better, had the perfect solution and could therefore solve all the customer's problems. Lucy made a mental note to consider how a customer might feel when she called them. Perhaps she would even ask someone.

The training droned on. It was delivered as a lecture with no reference to the individual's ability or experience. There seemed to be a million procedures and Lucy couldn't help thinking that the company had forgotten that it was meant to have a relationship with its customers. The breaks were fun though because ten boys and girls had such a wide range of experiences and they all enjoyed music, partying, cars and some even had their own home. Lucy returned to her hutch, invigorated. The training droned on, blah, blah, blah, 'smile as you dial'. She decided the company expected the customer to fall in line with their own procedures and Lucy was glad to go home, but she had high hopes for the week ahead. She just wanted to get on the phone.

They were to spend the week at the impersonal training hutches and those who passed the test at the end of the week would be allowed upstairs. Some of the career sales advisers groaned at the mention of a test. Lucy assumed that they hadn't planned on going back to school but it was familiar territory to her, so she looked forward to it.

Lucy had seen upstairs on her first day. Because she was so early there was no one to meet her so she had gone up there by mistake and seen the wide expanse of carefully-planned work stations. It had a clean, efficient and purposeful feel about it and the guys who had helped her find the training room had been very friendly and helpful. It felt like home and Lucy visualised herself up there, really talking to customers; but she kept this thought to herself.

The script was tailor-made for a compliant customer and Lucy role-played at tables for four where they pitched and re-pitched to each other, breaking down into hysterics when it went wrong; and it went wrong a lot!

Lucy got it pretty quickly. She was used to doing what she was told but two of her group were failing miserably. Lucy felt bad thinking it, but, it was almost as though they couldn't even read properly. She felt really sorry for them; after all, someone had recruited them – hadn't they thought to ask basic, relevant questions?

From their conversations at break-time, Lucy began to doubt their motivation. Several of the boys laughed about selling anything they liked to customers who didn't want it and in some cases, couldn't even use it. Clothes, watches and cars were high on their list of aspirations and Lucy felt a little sick to be part of a profession that was encouraged to set simple material goals like that. So, in her mind, some of her colleagues deserved to suffer at the role play table, so when she was receiving a call from one she did not approve of, Lucy gave them a particularly complicated scenario which quickly stumped them and made them look foolish. Lucy apologised but was secretly pleased and had the feeling that several others in her group appreciated what she was doing.

The trainer seemed oblivious to what was going on. It seemed as though she had never made a sales call in her life which was a shame, because Lucy wanted to ask if there was one perfect voice for telephone selling.

AUTHOR'S NOTE

Lucy is delighted to be accepted by a brand-named corporation because she can rely on them to play by the rules and therefore start to make plans. She is a little surprised by the wide range of abilities accepted by the company but recognises that the cloning process will reject those that don't fit. Lucy is thrilled to be one of the best but she is more excited to recognise an opportunity to improve the customer experience.

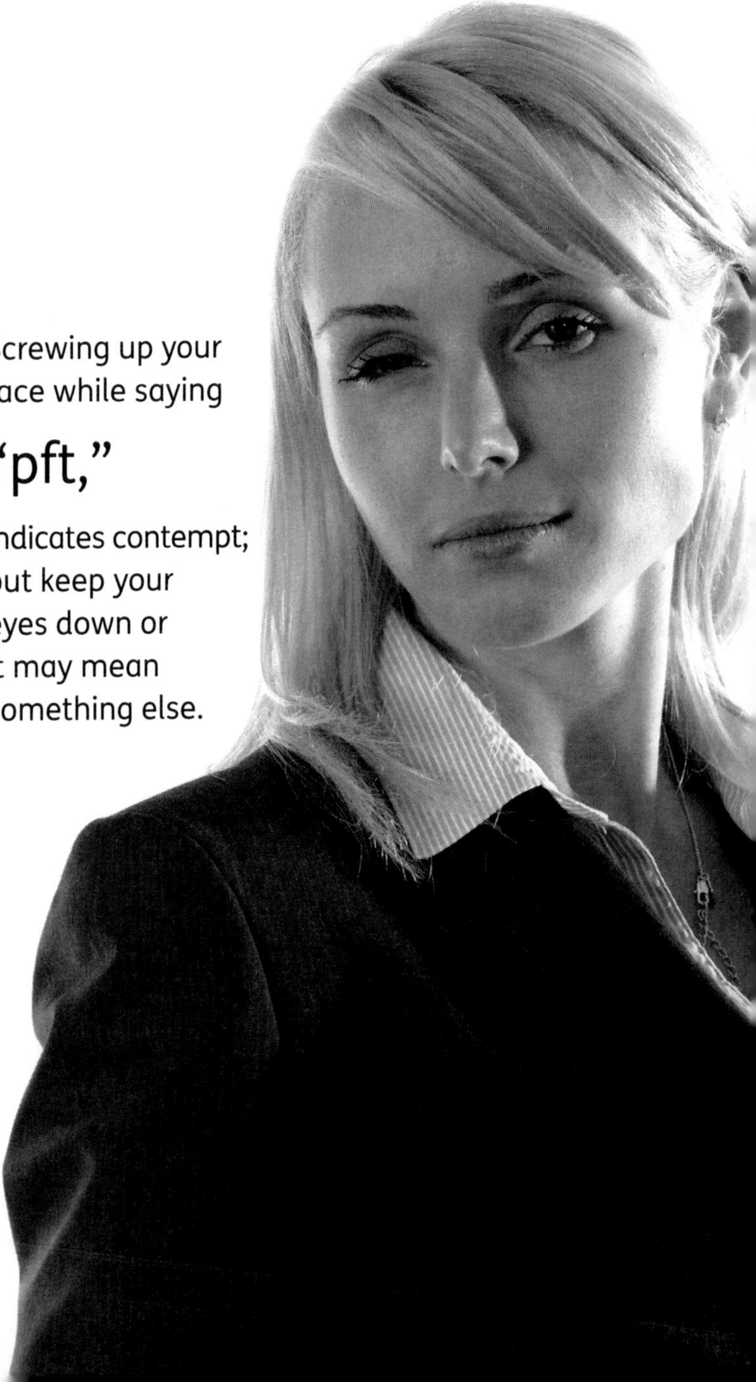

Screwing up your face while saying

"pft,"

indicates contempt; but keep your eyes down or it may mean something else.

11. Contempt

The five that had made it upstairs were proud of themselves and put on an air of confidence but on the inside, they were trembling like jellies. To be among the smart, purposeful and successful telephone sellers was awe-inspiring. Lucy was wearing her smartest business suit, the one she had bought when she went shopping with Natalie, and she could tell that the others were at their smartest too except one chap, Julian, who had on an old suit, un-ironed shirt and trainers.

Alex, their new team leader, welcomed them to the 'incubator' and gave them a guided tour of the various teams, toilets and cafe where there was a range of seating and tables that spoke of commitment to the telephone sales advisers. Lucy was, however, a little disappointed when Alex showed them to a row of six hutches which were only marginally larger than those for the training. He sat at the end and they all faced the team of new recruits from the week before. She could see four more rows of hutches in front of her which she calculated would take her ten weeks to negotiate. A computer and phone took up most of her space and she could see that no-one had tried to personalise their space.

By lunchtime she was familiar with how the script integrated with her auto-dialler and various quotation and purchasing screens. Alex announced that, after lunch, they would make a call, one at a time, and evaluate each other as they went along. He was very fair and at exactly two o'clock, made the first call.

The system made a connection based on a process of ongoing information messages previously dialled and he concluded his call by selling holiday insurance to an existing mortgage customer. Lucy noted that the potential customer had been almost pleased to hear from him and she silently questioned how easy it had been for Alex to start the conversation and ask questions in comparison to the cold calls she had made for Martin and Ester.

They all applauded Alex and concluded that he had stuck to the script and routed perfectly thus justifying his reward. Commission would not be a consideration until they had graduated from the incubator. Lucy added that Alex had sounded concerned for the customer but he dismissed her comment saying: "We always need to be concerned, Lucy."

Steven was clearly the most qualified of their group, having worked in mobile phone sales for four years. His experience on the next call was not so satisfactory because the customer kept interrupting him, which unnerved him to the point where he lost his place and had to end the call unsatisfactorily. Fortunately, he saved the day by saying to the customer: "I'm sorry, it's my first day." Everyone laughed and Alex delivered a short lecture about sticking to the script. Julian with the old suit was next, and Lucy could tell that Alex didn't approve.

Instead of saying "Hello," which was on the script, Alex said "Hi," and without a word of introduction, he went straight to the purpose of his call. Although the customer was friendly, she was taken by surprise at his blatant request for a commitment, even though it was in return for more insurance.

Julian ended the call with a request for an email which he seemed pleased about; but everyone was silent while Alex asked him to go downstairs to be enrolled on the next suitable training date. It seemed clear to Lucy that he wouldn't be given another date which was a shame, because she could see that Julian was trying to adapt the model to suit the customer; but he had failed, and now it was her turn to call.

She was pleased to hear a lady answer, a friendly Northerner who reminded her of her Aunt Denise. Lucy imagined that they were having a cosy chat on the sofa, as she did with her aunt, and read from the script as best she could. It was clear that the lady had only the minimum insurance but a large mortgage with the company. Lucy ascertained that her husband was away a lot, consulting, and she didn't like to make decisions like this on her own; so Lucy was pleased to agree that she try again next week when her husband would be home.

Alex wasn't so pleased. "Where on the script does it say that we will call back when the husband returns?" he asked ominously. Lucy was amazed. She knew that if she had pushed for the business they would probably have nothing and may even have earned themselves a bad name. Her colleagues all agreed that she had made a good call and that she sounded really friendly. Alex summarised by saying: "We always need to be friendly." Lucy wondered why Alex was the level one team leader of the incubator.

The two young boys were next. One had been selling cars and the other, Simon, had been an estate agent. They both closed small sales which were announced to the whole floor and met with cheers and a pat on the back from the incubator manager. Lucy collared Simon on the way out that evening. She had an inkling that he fancied her and so she was going to exchange her proximity with him for some of his steely determination. He was clearly delighted with the deal and invited her to have a cup of coffee with him. Lucy didn't like to drink caffeine after four o'clock so she had a camomile tea but Simon had two really relevant stories for her.

When he had been selling offices and warehouses in the Hammersmith area of London he had eventually extracted an offer for a warehouse that had been on the market for seven years. The offer had been for seventy thousand pounds per annum and Simon had taken the offer directly to his boss, Monty, who was a wizened old Londoner who knew the route and times for most buses in and out of the West End. Monty told Simon to call the client but added that he should report the offer at sixty thousand pounds per annum, ten thousand less. Simon had opened his mouth to question the behaviour but Monty had raised his index finger and said "Ah ah, just do it!" Simon had done as he was told and the client had complimented him on finally getting an offer, but told him to ask the potential tenant for eighty thousand pounds per annum. Simon hadn't stopped to think and reported what had happened to Monty, who told him to wait a day and call again to report the full, original offer. Simon did as he was told and the client gladly accepted the original offer, complimenting Simon on his negotiation skills. Simon told the new tenant the good news, documented the deal and earned his commission.

"What does it mean?" asked Lucy. "Clearly," said Simon, looking very pleased with himself, "that customers aren't interested in the facts, they are only interested in a result that suits them. I suppose that I could have kept negotiating and squeezed more out of the potential tenant but he may not have been happy with the deal and undoubtedly would have caused our client trouble in the long run. We created a win, win, win scenario for tenant, owner and us. Oh, and me too! Add another win to my list," he chuckled.

Lucy liked the sound of this but couldn't quite make sense of it. "What is the other story?" she asked, moving carefully to waft her perfume in Simon's direction. "Ah," said Simon, "this was my first deal, on my first day."

"I was given a dusty, buff coloured file for a factory in a real backwater. As I was given the file, I could hear sniggers from the secretaries. Looking back, this was my baptism of fire. No-one had tried to sell it for eighteen months and enquires had stopped when the advertising was pulled, so I flicked through the file, wondering what the heck I could do. There were some names and numbers on slips in the back of the file so I just called them and talked to local businessmen who were still interested but had assumed it had been sold. Anyway, to cut a long story short, I ended up calling one then another all afternoon. It felt like trading on the stock market and the price rose from seventy five thousand pounds to one hundred and thirty thousand pounds. The client was over the moon and I earned my badge of honour." "What did that teach you?" asked Lucy. "Well, I felt a bit guilty playing one off against the other and I told this to the 'big cheese' who I bumped into while making coffee but he said to me – and I shall never forget these words: "In sales, son, sometimes you have to be a little selfish." "Whoa!" said Lucy. "These are great lessons. Thank you, Simon."

"C'mon you two," said the incubator manager. "We are all going home and we don't even wait for keen bees." They both took this as a major compliment and shuffled out alongside the senior sellers, feeling very grown up. Simon asked her to join him for a pizza but Lucy had had enough of him and excused herself, quoting exercise as her reason, which it was.

AUTHOR'S NOTE

While Lucy is prepared to do as she is told, she is also eager to take risks and improve as fast as possible. She analyses behaviour that works well and not so well and is willing to do what it takes to access valuable information. She is delighted to recognise that a simple story is a powerful sales tool.

You can hear a

“growl”

and see it in her eyes. She is spurred on to take a risk and improve her own performance.

12. Anger

Lucy sat in her hutch. She had managed to be really early again but she pledged to time it better soon and use the buses next week. She was the first of her team in and there were only a couple of others in what looked like week three and five hutches. A fat woman was trying to sort out armfuls of paperwork. Lucy hated fat people, not because they were fat, that wouldn't be, fair but because they often acted like losers, not doing things because they were fat. Having thought about it, Lucy hated people who acted like losers. In her opinion they were weak, and all too ready to compromise. The other was a young man with his feet up on the back of another chair while listening to The Beatles on his iPod. Lucy wondered how he could make good sales calls. He must be half deaf from listening at that volume. She wandered away from the incubator, trying desperately not to look like she was prying, or planning to steal anything, but she couldn't quite work out how that body language should be, so she tried to look casual. She was sure that she did, in her smart black trousers and cream silk top.

It was the corporate art on the wall she was interested in – not exactly interested in, but interested to see. Like Beatles boy, she had an urge to 'own her space.' She had brought in a few adornments for her desk but wasn't convinced that Alex would allow it, so she decided to play that situation by ear. The art looked like a carpet because it was textured and the pattern made her think of Africa and the colours made her think of poor people.

"It looks like a computer chip doesn't it." Lucy jumped. Alex had sneaked up behind her. "Oooh, you frightened me," she chastised. "Sorry, but you shouldn't be over here," said Alex. "C'mon, come back to the best place in the world." Lucy smiled and thought that he may not be a bad team leader after all. "A computer chip, you say?" said Lucy. "Oh yeah, a really powerful, futuristic computer chip," said Alex. "Interesting," said Lucy, wondering how they could have such extremely different opinions of something so bland.

Everyone was in just before nine and on the dot, Alex announced: "Today, I want all of you to make one hundred calls. All you have to do is let the system make the connections for you and stick to the script." He almost shouted this last bit. "You will not be invited back if you don't do this today. Now, get on the phones and make those calls." There were a few muttered swear words and a lot of frenetic fiddling with headsets, adjustment of seats and logging on. Lucy hunkered down, thinking: "This is ridiculous. It may be a good test of our commitment to the company but the only people who will suffer are the customers." She logged on anyway and told herself that she would 'see what happens'.

The range of customer circumstances was astounding to Lucy. She wondered about the company's target marketing strategy as she spoke to people with tiny mortgages, lots of insurance and huge loans to people with no loans, no insurance and huge mortgages. They all had a different sound which fascinated Lucy and she naturally adapted to their pace, tone and timing. Sticking to the script was a pain but she kept at it because Alex was pacing behind them, urging them on like a captain to his gunners in an old-fashioned sea battle. He picked on everyone if they deviated but Lucy was sure that several potential customers were put off buying by her inability to speak naturally. Very few sales had been made by lunchtime but everyone had made a good number of calls so, they adjourned for lunch five minutes early to beat the queue.

Lucy was sure that there were several customers who would have bought from her if she had spoken naturally to them and she was worried that the brain-washing Alex was enforcing on them was going to spoil her ability to really connect with people.

"It's so safe, isn't it?" said Beatles boy, who had taken out his earphones as he saw Lucy approaching with her tray. "Can I share your table?" she asked. He agreed nonchalantly and was going to put his earphones back in when Lucy asked: "What do you mean, it's safe?" "Safe for the company to have us all stick to the same script. In a way, it's reassuring." "Do you have to stick to it as well, in, what are you, week five?" "I'm afraid so, but we have more products to offer so it gets easier and we are measured on a combination of dials and sales agreed," he said proudly. Lucy felt a bit sick.

She wanted to take risks, play with what she said and experiment with the customers' reaction until she learned their language. "How could the company decide that everyone required the same options during a conversation?" she wondered. Lucy had already recognised that customers with very similar circumstances could have completely different attitudes to the company. One chose it because it represented a safe pair of hands but another because they believed it to have a risk friendly investment strategy.

"What do you like about The Beatles?" she asked. "How do you know I like them?" He looked a little shocked. "I could hear it a mile off," she told him. "'She loves you, yeah, yeah, yeah!'" what does that mean?" challenged Lucy. "Well," he said, taking his time, "it means that the girl of my dreams is out there waiting to love me." "What is love to you?" asked Lucy. "You know, commitment and marriage," was the rather humble response she received. Lucy was a little in awe of his answer because it wasn't one she felt comfortable challenging but she knew in her heart that she didn't know what love was. She had heard it described as 'friendship on fire' and she understood that but surely, this was a description of passion or perhaps lust. It was interesting that some words seemed to mean anything to anyone and this was the risk they were not being allowed to use on the phones.

That afternoon, she put her head down, turned her brain onto dormant and made four sales from fifty-eight calls. She was pleased that Alex was happy but she was also pleased for James, the ex car salesman and the youngest of their group, who had made an amazing one hundred and twenty-eight calls that day but no sales.

On day three, Alex was sick, so another team leader announced that week one was all about one hundred calls per day; but he was more interested in his own team's performance so Lucy decided to try a different way. In her opinion, the problem was that most customers believed they didn't want to hear from the company; but Lucy considered this to be a learned reaction because telephone sales still had a fairly bad reputation. They had all disapproved of Julian in his scruffy suit but to Lucy's mind, he may have been the best among them if he was given the chance.

Tough customers, who amounted to about half of their connections, sounded quite impervious as the script routed them through a series of statements and questions that were designed to soften them up, but they rarely reacted to this fairly blatant tactic.

Lucy remembered that when she was in a bad mood, and Jack tried to bring her out of it with jokes and kindness, it would always take him longer than if he played grumpy, too; so Lucy tried mirroring her tough customers' behaviour and introduced a few lines about how she wasn't doing too well either, how she hated her job, her flat or her boyfriend. The others were giving her some really strange looks but her replacement team leader hadn't noticed because he was busy marking up his own teams' dials for the day on their whiteboard.

Lucy was amazed at how well the tough ones reacted to her new approach and nearly all of them were more willing to chat with her; but she had nowhere to go with her new-found acquaintance because the script started pushing product and as friendly as these new acquaintances were, they were still wary of being sold something over the phone.

It was like a 'Them verses the Company' battle and Lucy felt as though she was standing between two opposing armies.

A few were even rude to her but she considered this to be evidence that she was getting somewhere and by the end of the day, she had earned herself the second most sales after Steven, who had stuck to the script; but Lucy knew she that she had acquired a more powerful process for the future.

We are all a product of our environment

AUTHOR'S NOTE

Lucy has recognised that customers have a particular sound. She realises that it may be based on their learned behaviour so goes on to test her theory that if she mirrors their pace, tone and timing, they often change that behaviour. By doing this, she has made her sales calls slightly more enjoyable for her customers but realises that something is missing.

If you think and say

"Ooh, that's nice"

your potential customer can enjoy the process, too.

13. Sensual Pleasure

Alex was back the next day and congratulated them all except Simon, who was struggling with the discipline of constant repetition. "I feel like a victim," he told Lucy during a break.

They all, however, made it to week two and a new team leader, who introduced them to payment protection insurance and monetary targets. They were expected to make five sales a day which at least took the pressure off volume dialling; but Lucy couldn't stop thinking about the corporate art. Alex had seen a micro chip and she had seen a carpet. Why? How? Beatles boy thought love was all about commitment and marriage but she thought it might just be passion and lust. How did that happen "Why do similar people have such different opinions of the same thing?" she wondered. "Surely the company's customers had different opinions of insurance and PPI?" She knew a lot of people who hated it but perhaps that was their learned behaviour. If only she could get into their heads. She could compare their relationship with what she was selling and the sound they made. But how?

The answer hit her like a wall of cold air as she was driving in on a wet day. She just wasn't going to battle for the bus on a day like this. The journey was taking a lot longer than usual. Lucy presumed it was because the torrential rain forced other bus users and cyclists into their cars too. As a consequence she was playing a tune which she loved, by The Pussycat Dolls, again and again. The lyrics were lovely. It was about the ongoing search for the right man who would have his own business, house, cars and money but still have some time for her while she furthered her own reputation until they decided, jointly, to have children. To Lucy, "I must stick wid' you forever," was a metaphor for the right guy and not one person. "Nobody gonna take me higher," meant that he would add to her own reputation and possibly fame. But when she listened to it for the ninth or tenth time she began to pull the words apart and realise that if she hadn't been so lucky in life, it might mean sticking with one guy and great sex. "So, if I could introduce this sort of audience-specific language into the conversation with a potential customer, they might tell me their own interpretation of what I want to talk about," she thought.

In an excited frame of mind she ran the idea by her new team leader. He seemed to get it but asked her in a rather patronising tone: "So, what happens next?" Lucy hadn't really thought about that. "Well, we offer them the relevant product, you know, in accordance with what they tell us," she answered. "What do you mean?" asked the manager, rather cynically. "I don't know," said Lucy, defeated. She put her head down for the day and received her pat on the back for dedication and making five sales. It was funny how everyone did what they had to do and no more.

With nothing to do that rainy night and little on the telly, Lucy decided to listen to the afternoon play on the internet. The play was written in the style of a documentary about couples speed dating and then it tracked their relationship over the next few months. Lucy realised that you could predict which couples would succeed by the tone of their voice. If a man sounded a little guarded and a woman open to ideas, that worked, and vice a versa. Surprisingly, if they both sounded matter of fact that worked, too; but if one sounded matter of fact and the other guarded or open to new ideas, that seemed to fail. "So, if I am able to say something that is open to interpretation in a way that compliments my customers sound, our relationship might be good enough to encourage them to tell me about their relationship with what I am selling," she thought.

Lucy had the bit firmly between her teeth now. She knew the feeling. Her parents laughed about how determined she was as a child. One Christmas, she had been given a pair of Barbie roller blades and she would have skipped Christmas lunch if she had been allowed to. Clunk, clunk, clunk. All day she had tried and tried until she could glide smoothly around her Grandpa's drive. She would have carried on learning to do jumps and spins if they had had a good enough porch light as it went dark. Several summers before she had decided not to go to her first school disco just so that she could master her new skipping rope.

Today was a day for the bus and she queued, hardly noticing the world around her because she was living in a world of customer interaction. The bus stop stank because an old tramp was slumped in a corner and he looked to be in a really bad way. As Lucy joined the queue she couldn't help voicing her displeasure at the smell and that seemed to spur the others into action. A smartly dressed man crouched down and asked the tramp directly, "What's your name? What's your name?" He shouted the second request but the tramp didn't flinch, he totally ignored the man. The group re-gathered its senses and a lady in a smart suit, cagoule and sandals bent down and said: "My name is Moira Newman and I am the secretary at the Muddylane Men's Working Club. What is your name please?" The tramp raised his head with tears in his eyes and told her. He wasn't well and the problem wasn't fundamentally drink so they called him an ambulance. Moira stayed with him to allow the others to get on with their day.

Lucy had learned that you have to pitch to win permission to ask questions.

Lucy had been doing five sales a day easily and her colleagues had kept up, except young James who sounded so, well, young. Their team leader was quite comfortable that they were hitting target and didn't seem to expect any more. Anyway, he was working closely with James so Lucy had time to experiment. So far she had found out that when she made seventy five calls a day, about fifty would let her go through the introduction; but when she wanted to ask the questions only five of them would let her and they, so far, had all agreed to some sort of deal for the whiteboard. So, by Lucy's calculation, ninety three percent of potential customers needed something different to the rigid script the company seemed to love so much.

With four sales on the board before lunch, Lucy prepared to try something new that afternoon. During lunch she took a prime position at the communal table, which was frequented by those who wanted a quick snack so that they could go shopping, read a magazine or do a job as well during their break. Lucy took advantage of the situation and managed to ask nine people what one word they would relate to the company's attitude to customers. The most common word was 'caring' so Lucy put it into a sentence after introducing herself on the phone. By the end of the afternoon she calculated that twenty percent had let her go through to the questions, which meant that she had doubled her conversation rate.

Her dad was in high spirits when she got in. He was having one of his poker nights with his pals and that usually meant beer, whisky and smoking. Lucy planned to keep out of the way but it was impossible when she needed to cook. With a pan of noodles on the hob, she couldn't avoid an olive-skinned 'know it all' called Gunter. "Hey, how are you doing Lucy?" he asked. "Fine, thank you," she said. "How are you?" "Really great, thanks. Are you working now?" Lucy knew she wasn't going to be able to avoid a full conversation with this guy so she decided to make the best of it because, to be fair, he did have a lot of sensible opinions. She told him everything that had happened over the past two weeks and she could tell he was impressed; but he was a little tipsy so all he said was "Hey, it's all about Transactional Analysis." Lucy hadn't a clue what he was talking about and dismissed his comment as the sort of crap all her dad's pals came out with around her.

By lunchtime the next day she had marked up her four sales and in the afternoon, planned to try out her new idea again. At lunch, she took her place at the communal table and found out that eleven different people thought happy customers would say that the company offered a better than average return on savings. Lucy didn't think that this was particularly impressive but her potential customers obviously did because by the end of the day, twenty-five per cent had spoken to her and she had agreed two more sales, which made her the first in her group to do one hundred and twenty per cent of her daily sales target.

At the end of the week, Lucy was given a bottle of company champagne as a prize for being best new performer. She hoped the others didn't hate her for it and offered to share it, which they did, in plastic cups, and agreed to go to the pub. Lucy wasn't great at small talk. Her friends described her as driven, which was the compliment; but the fact that she was driven was also her weakness. The chatter about work and office politics changed to more general subjects, so she nursed her drink.

An older guy in a classy suit manoeuvred himself in front of her and asked: "Do you fancy a chat?" What could she say? He was clearly willing to be entertaining, was good looking – and she did love his suit. He had a lot to say about work, sport and food and Lucy was happy to enjoy the show. He asked her about what she did and she told him. "Oh, you're one of those?" he said. "What do you mean by that?" asked Lucy, crossly. "Well," said Mike, "in 2008." Lucy thought, "when I was studying at university," He went on: "I took a call from this guy who wouldn't take no for an answer." Lucy thought, "well I would take no for an answer." He went on again: "and I had a movie on pause and dinner in the microwave." "I would have asked," thought Lucy. "So," he said, "I just put down the phone." "How embarrassing," said Lucy, "you don't think I'm one of those do you?" "Well," said Mike, a little sheepishly, "You're all the same aren't you?"

In response, she said: "To be fair, I hear a lot of telephone sales are done badly but in my opinion, it can be done well. So well, in fact, that it becomes enjoyable for the customer, profitable for our bosses and sustainable for the poor saps who are currently treated like cannon fodder." "Whoa!" said Mike. "Have I touched a raw nerve?" "I suppose you have," said Lucy. "Do you want to discuss it over dinner?" asked Mike. "Why not," replied Lucy.

Mike was a life insurance salesman and he offered Lucy a position at his company on better pay; but she would have to make calls on her own, surrounded by others not making calls, and Lucy was already wise enough to know that having just one person in a group not making calls sapped energy like a black hole. She could imagine how bad it would be to be surrounded by everyone not making calls, listening and evaluating her every action. "What would they make of the risks I want to take?" she wondered. She thanked him, but declined on the basis that she wanted to stick with the company's training programme. Mike, however, had a decent philosophy about sales. He did a lot of business networking so had plenty of opportunities to connect with potential customers; but from what he told her sheunderstood that he went straight to the product facts and figures, which Lucy now wholeheartedly thought was wrong.

He said that there were three types of buyer: those who wanted insurance immediately, those who didn't and those who were worth keeping in touch withbecause they were willing to have their relationship with insurance understood. Apparently, ten per cent bought immediately and another ten percent were interesting enough to keep in touch with. Lucy knew he could increase the second category but she kept this to herself for now. She accepted his offer of a lift home and was glad that her dad was there on her arrival. It avoided any complications and she dismissed Mike with a promise to call him next time she was hungry.

The weekend was beautiful and Lucy dedicated it to the beach, reading and research. Transactional Analysis was a theory about the three human ego states. It explained her recognition that people sounded either cautious, matter of fact or open to new ideas, and described these states as parent, adult or child ego states.

Week three moved them to a new row of hutches, another team leader and another product. James had left or been pushed because there were only places for four now, and one was for the team leader; but these hutches were larger; they were almost desk-sized and Lucy remembered that she had planned to ask Alex about personalising her space. Somehow, her new plan to improve calls was more important now, so she put her back into her work and made all but one of her targeted calls by lunchtime. "I've noticed," said the new team leader, Neil, "that you do really well in the morning and quite poorly in the afternoon." "Blast," thought Lucy. "I've been rumbled." But she wasn't going to give up without a fight so she gave Neil a full introduction to her childhood, lifestyle and metabolism, concluding that, as a female, she had no alternative. He swallowed the confusion and looked impressed and Lucy was delighted to be allowed to continue.

At lunch, she took her place at the communal table and asked about ten people if they could quote any results or performance that customers could rely on. The most common answer was that because the company's market share grew year on year, they had begun to 'make the market'. Lucy had no idea what this meant but her potential customers loved it, and she increased her conversation rate to thirty percent and made four sales that afternoon. Neil was very pleased with himself, thinking that he was the catalyst for the improvement. Lucy knew differently.

AUTHOR'S NOTE

Lucy has become defensive of telephones sales, recognising that it can be done well, and she is developing a pitch based on audience-specific language made up of an abstract noun, a short story and quotable results. She is using this language to get her customers to talk openly about their relationship with what she is selling, which earns her permission to ask relevant questions.

"Wahey!"

shouted Lucy as
she punched the air,
partly in relief.

14. Freedom

Lucy liked being in control, it made her feel a little like a predator instead of prey. In her opinion, it was her life and she had only one of them, so she was damn well going to make the most of it. If that caused others to disapprove, so be it. They could sack her for all she cared. She was only trying to do it better and allow the customers to enjoy the interaction. Using her audience-specific language, however, required her to 'let go' during a call to someone she had never met and couldn't see, and that was a frightening prospect. It felt like stepping into the void for a parachute jump. You got that stomach-twisting empty feeling that told you not to do it. It was so unnatural but she needed to conquer her fear and she looked forward to her parachute opening.

So far, Lucy had recognised that selling insurance and PPI was like a box-ticking exercise. Only those who recognised that they needed it bought it; but Lucy had introduced emotion into the buying process. If you love yourself, your family and your house, you would insure it. If you love the status quo, you would insure that too. The trouble was, Lucy had only experienced the free-falling part of her parachute jump. She now had her hand on the rip cord, so to speak, but the chute was yet to billow open and she therefore hadn't experienced finding out what customers loved about the effects of insurance.

Over the next few days her conversation rate fluctuated but her sales remained on target. Whatever she did, wherever she went, she was looking for something but she wasn't sure what. Life wasn't the same for her anymore. In a way, she had added another dimension to her world and she was determined that she wouldn't let herself relax until she had found the solution.

There was something very satisfying about recycling. Her dad had a big bag in a cupboard into which they threw bottles, cans and plastics, once clean. There was a shelf for paper and cardboard too. They were both quite inventive about how they recycled: toilet rolls would be creased, cut and flattened out and large plastic containers would be cut up, so each segment would concertina into the other. In a crazy way, they were both proud to put out a tiny amount of rubbish for the bin men on Thursday. "I have to get my own place," Lucy chuckled to herself but in her heart she knew she would adopt the same procedure in a flat of her own.

It wasn't necessarily the recycling that gave her pleasure, or even minimising her use of council resources, but the fact that it was one small step towards connecting with the planet and in a twenty first century sort of way, harmonising her interaction with nature.

"Would you help me sell barn dance tickets please, sweetheart?" asked her dad. He was a member of the local tennis club. The standard of tennis was appalling, proved by the fact that they hadn't won a single match in ten years; but her dad was captain of the new men's team and he was determined to make something of it. For some reason, he felt that making himself accountable for the barn dance would be the first step towards success for the club. She knew he said that he simply enjoyed a good barn dance but she also knew that he would do everything necessary to make it a success because he cared; so she would care, too.

Lucy announced to her team that she was selling tickets to a barn dance but only received sniggers and derision. "Oh yeah, I love a good doh see doh," said Steven, suggestively. "Well, it's your loss," replied Lucy, knowing in her heart that it really was something they would regret not doing. At the break, she considered that there was a job to be done so she approached Beatles boy and asked him what he did after work. He was happy to tell her about his record collection, how he was ashamed to be still living with his mum and his passion for football. Lucy asked him if he ever went to pubs and clubs but he didn't because he considered them a place where fake friendship was all you got, if at all. She asked him about dancing and he was clearly enjoying her questions so he told her about his salsa dance classes, a trip to Bolivia and his lapsed membership of a Ceroc Club. So Lucy told him what she liked about barn dancing and her dad's event coming up. He was very keen and bought a ticket immediately, and Lucy wondered at the process of questions that had made closing the deal such a natural thing to do.

On one level, they were both looking forward to a barn dance but on the other level, she had made a sale. Lucy immediately asked the same questions of a young man in week five but he wasn't keen to answer her.

The floor manager regularly received parcels at his station towards the end of the sales floor and they could all see this activity and watched it with interest, because the parcels contained the cleansed data from head office that they all used to make their sales calls.

For some reason, over the past few days, all the team leaders had been comparing their virility, measuring it by the number of children they had spawned. They had even started a leader's board and while most had one or two children, several had none and one chap had five. This fascination had turned into a small-scale anthropology study and they had added some external data; so when the next parcel arrived, the floor manager signed for it and asked the courier: "How many kids do you have, my friend?" The courier gave the floor manager a very strange look and said: 'That's my business, mate" and turned his back to walk away. The floor manager shrugged off the rebuttal and later that day tried again; but it was significant to note that this time he signed for the parcel, told the courier about their study – and then asked. An answer was forthcoming and Lucy remembered the tramp.

At lunch, an acquaintance of Beatles boy approached her and asked if it was she who was selling tickets to a barn dance. Lucy didn't go straight for the kill this time. She had learned her lesson. She told him a little about it and asked about his life and relationship with dance and only then asked if he wanted a ticket. "Oh yes," he said. "I'll take four please." Lucy was a little taken aback. By pitching him and asking relevant questions she had converted someone she didn't know into someone who she had a relationship with and then into a customer; and he had enjoyed the buying process, too.

She made a note to try this on the phone. What she needed was relevant but indirect questions.

The weather was mild but there was a blustery wind with rain in the air. Lucy felt a little trapped by spending so much time in the office but she knew that a run would blow away the cobwebs. As she stepped outside in her running vest and shorts she felt the cold rain smacking her hard in the wind and reconsidered her plan. She hated this part of a run but she knew how she would feel when it was over; so she stretched, and started breathing deeply.

She got going, slowly at first, knowing she would build up to a fast run, verging on a sprint. Her long legs let her fly along and the blustery wind excited her around her new route. This was a moment to forget all her troubles and concentrate on her body as a machine, working in perfect harmony to take in air and convert every available micron of energy into propulsion.

As she was stretching out she wondered at how she now considered the air to be warm and caressing even though she was soaked to the skin by sweat and rain. She wondered how long she would continue to run like this, how old would she be before she had to give up and would that time be extended by the fact she did it? She concluded that she ran for the immediate and obvious benefit of suppleness and finding everyday life easy in comparison but also, perhaps, for the longer term benefit of extended life. “How well does the phrase ‘keep fit’ really represent all these considerations,” she mused.

Back at work, she continued to take risks ‘off script’ as soon as she gauged that her team leader was otherwise engaged. She mirrored the sound of each potential customer, asked for permission to tell them her exciting reason for the call and told them about other customers, why they liked the company and the results they were proud of. She grinned because now she knew what to do; so she asked about their behaviour with regard to finance, their environment – which included home, work and family – and then she asked about their skills or experience of finance. They were clearly enjoying answering these questions and when she came to closing the sale, it seemed painless. It even felt a little like she was doing them a favour and Lucy ended the day with double her quota of targeted sales and a strange feeling of power.

Barn dance tickets were selling like hot cakes now and Lucy was consistently top sales adviser. Her new-found formula was giving her celebrity status in the office but she felt that there was more to be done on the phone. When she asked for permission to pitch and used her audience-specific language, she naturally did it with an open mind so while this process was effective, it required a lot of effort because the customers rarely sounded cheerful and that bothered her.

She only recognised this now that the office seemed like a cheerful environment to her. Her colleagues were in awe of her results and the management was clearly proud of her, her sales and her 'call to sale' ratio. One sale in five calls was unheard of but she really was engaging and building rapport so well that one in five customers bought something. The only problem was that because she was wrapping up so many sales, her call volume had declined to around forty five calls per day. Personally, Lucy was happy with this because, in her mind, that was a sustainable number but she was worried because it was so far off what the company demanded.

On the last day of her induction, the floor manager called her over to the conference room. Lucy wasn't sure whether to be excited or frightened. He was about forty-five years old and seemed huge to Lucy with greying black hair. She had received occasional nods and grunts from him which she considered to be a great favour, because he only ever spoke to the team leaders. Everyone referred to him as 'boss'.

He was seated when she entered the room and he gestured her to a chair. He had the reputation of being a fabulous telephone sales adviser and Lucy wondered why he didn't ever make any calls. "Hello, Lucy," he said and she immediately knew why he didn't make any calls. His voice had a really high pitch, almost like a girl,

"My name is Robert, Robert Pink." Lucy relaxed, something told her this was going to be a good meeting. "I am pleased to meet you Mr Pink," said Lucy. "Robert, please," he said. "Err, Robert," said Lucy. "Now, we have recognised your good work but we have a dilemma. You see, we demand, and you know we demand, that everyone sticks to the script and makes one hundred calls per day and you haven't been doing that, have you Lucy?"

Lucy was crestfallen. At first, she was sure they would be monitoring her calls and she was scared to run her first few trials 'off script'; but after a few weeks and many days of not ever using the script, she had assumed they would let it go – especially as she had been producing such great results. "Obviously not," she thought; but there was something about his attitude that made her feel brave. She wasn't going to apologise and she decided on the spot that she wasn't going back to using the script, whatever the consequences. "No," she said. "I don't think the script works well for me or the customer or you." "Are you challenging our company policy, Lucy?" he asked abruptly. Lucy had to think. This meeting was getting rapidly out of hand so she muttered to herself 'let's see what happens' and launched, not into a challenge, but into some beautifully crafted audience-specific language.

"Robert, when I joined the company – and I want to thank you for giving me the opportunity to join such a wonderful company – I heard 'stick to the script' time and time again and how I interpreted that was 'satisfy our customers because without them we are nothing, and when we get them on our side they make us profitable' and that, as you know, is what I have been doing – better than most. But if you have to sack me for doing my job well, that is your decision." She regretted adding these last words but stayed silent. He remained dead still and Lucy was a little frightened of what might happen. It seemed like an age until he spoke again and when he did, it was in a gruesomely dispassionate voice.

"Lucy," he said, "I'm afraid I am going to have to let you go." She couldn't believe it. Had she misjudged his behaviour so badly? Obviously she had but she had never pleaded in her life and she wasn't going to start now, so she stood up, offered her hand and said: "I respect your decision Robert but I am not comfortable that the company is so fixed in their ways that they wouldn't change their policy to serve customers and employees better." "Hold on," he said. "Sit down. I'm going to have to let you go as a telephone sales adviser but if you believe wholeheartedly that you are doing the right thing, then I want to offer you a role in the training department."

In Lucy's opinion he had earned a hug and he got one – a big, childlike embrace that made him very aware of how grateful she was. They discussed terms and agreed that she would aim to convert telephone sales advisers into telephone sales consultants, a subtle change that would allow the sales team to shed their victim-like status and adopt that of a predator, albeit one with a farmer's mentality; and Robert walked back to his desk with four barn dance tickets in his breast pocket.

AUTHOR'S NOTE

Lucy has recognised that she can significantly improve her chances of making a sale by allowing the customer to put negative, learned behaviour aside. By pitching potential customers with audience-specific language, they often take ownership of the conversation and consider what she is selling, even if they weren't thinking about it before she called. Now she has recognised that by adding open, rapport-building questions based on behaviour, environment and skills, her customers are really enjoying the process, buying instead of her selling. All her hard work and determination seems to be paying off.

Your bottom lip
doubles up as
you nod and
tip your head
and hum

"hm,"

seeing your
idea adopted by
everyone else.

15. Pride

The average calls to sales ratio was ten in one hundred and naturally, the company wanted more; but this was not the issue as far as Lucy was concerned. Her primary concern was for the customers, who she knew did not enjoy being herded through the script. Her secondary concern was for her colleagues, who were dragged down by unhappy potential customers and a pressure to meet ever-changing targets.

The training team was like a different species and they greeted Lucy enthusiastically, showing her around, offering her coffee and explaining that her desk was among a group of six in the large office, which had a connecting door to the Training Director's room. It all seemed a little like a set-up and Lucy was cautious. They were so friendly and helpful. One tall, dark, handsome young man, Gethin, seemed to only just stop short of proposing marriage!

They seemed to want to extract every ounce of her knowledge but she didn't think she had enough; she had developed a system that worked for her but she didn't really know how to share it with others yet.

Lucy let them show her the training programmes which of course she was aware of because she had only recently been trained herself; but if she was honest, she hadn't really listened beyond day two. Lucy didn't like anyone telling her how to interact with people. She was the mistress of interaction and always had been.

Whenever her family went on holiday it was Lucy who brought new friends to their group or linked their group to another. There was an energy about her that no-one could explain but it was an energy that disappeared when she was alone. It was as though she fed off other people but in return, she would always pay them back by making them feel better about themselves. She was a human chameleon and Lucy knew that this was essentially how she made great sales calls. Some of her colleagues were brilliant on the phone but they only had one sound whereas Lucy had a wide range of sounds. Interestingly, she didn't enjoy making some of them and she put that down to her upbringing. She wasn't comfortable with the sounds that she wasn't familiar with but she was learning fast. All she had to do was help her colleagues be comfortable with this range of sounds, too. 'That's it," she thought. "The telephone sales advisers are my colleagues, not these trainers."

"Look, I'm sorry," she told them "I'm not a trainer, I am a telephone sales adviser and I cannot have been invited to join you just to continue what you are doing. I am going to try and do it my own way and if it fails, I can always go back on the phones." She knew she couldn't, not at this company anyway; but the trainers didn't know that and she had alienated herself so that she could get on with thinking about this afresh.

During her time on the phones, Lucy had worked out that it hardly mattered what you say. What mattered was how you said it. She wasn't sure why, but she knew her colleagues needed to learn to be brave and make a range of sounds that would satisfy most customers.

They had sold 125 tickets to the barn dance which meant that her dad's theory that 'all you need is a great band and everything will be fine' would be put to the test; but other members of the tennis club had decorated the hall beautifully, stew and ploughman's lunches were prepared in advance and bales of straw had been borrowed, giving the hall a really authentic feel. Lucy had sold half of the tickets and some of her university friends were coming to stay for the weekend, including Jack.

She was really excited as she waited at the station for Natalie and Liz to arrive and they hugged and kissed and cried as they stumbled over news of their new lives. Lucy knew what to do and she fuelled their storytelling while she listened attentively. She gave them a little guided tour of the town with emphasis on the miles of beautiful beach, but the girls were interested in the pubs and clubs and wanted to go dancing straight away; but it was early and Lucy was driving so they compromised with a bottle of wine, which they drank while sitting on the sand under a blanket. She wanted them all to have an early night so they could make the best of tomorrow so they packed up as dusk fell, went home for some food and talked until midnight.

Fortunately, they slept until ten and were fully refreshed when Jack arrived in Johno's car with Matty. Neither of the other boys had been able to find a job so they greeted the girls sheepishly. They all went to the beach cafe for an early lunch and the boys were delighted to find out that Liz didn't have a job either, so everyone relaxed while the jobless pulled apart the others' work stories. It was sunny and warm so they took the ferry across to Mudeford spit and spent the afternoon sunbathing and swimming; but at five they had to go so the girls would have enough time to enjoy getting ready while the boys played on the Wii.

It was odd to see six cowboys and Indians bundle into a taxi. Natalie and Liz looked very sexy in their cowboy hats, boots and checked shirts tied in a knot at their waist. At first glance, you saw five cowboys; but on close inspection, two were clearly not cowboys but very pretty girls.

Lucy was dressed as a squaw with flat sandals, suede leather dress with tassels and a feather in her hair. Jack didn't like her wearing makeup so she didn't but compromised with war paint. He didn't like the dishonestly of 'putting on your face' and didn't want Lucy to become unable to leave the house without it.

Once they had found a table, Lucy went around the hall saying "Hi" to her work colleagues. They were all astounded to see her out of her usual work clothes and were a little lost for words until she broke the ice and got them comfortable. She brought as many as she could back to her table to say "Hello" but her friends struggled to know what to say to older, working men and women and after a short while, Jack decided that it would be better for him to join her on her rounds, leaving the others to drink and gossip.

It didn't seem long before the band's caller started the dancing and Jack said to Lucy: "Let's dance." There was something odd about his request, it felt a little like a command to Lucy; but she complied and they had a great time.

She was aware that a lot of her male colleagues had their eye on her and as soon as the first dance ended, a young lad she hardly knew bounced up and announced that Lucy would have the next dance with him. As much as Lucy was grateful to him for turning up, she was here to enjoy herself too, and she didn't appreciate being told; so she retorted "Oh, will she?" which made a moment for Beatles boy to gallantly request, with a bow: "Would Lucy be so kind as to grant me the next dance?" Now that was a request she wouldn't refuse and she made a mental note of the three different approaches.

Everyone had a fantastic night and left the hall sweaty and exhausted. Natalie and Liz had danced with all the men between them and were in the mood to drink late into the night, but Lucy couldn't shake a certain thought from her head. Even at a social event with such an emphasis on community, they were essentially selling themselves all the time.

Back at work on Monday, Lucy announced, among the thanks and accolades, that she was going to run a series of workshops like they had never experienced before. She wasn't going to force her script on them but they were going to be encouraged to look at themselves and make a change at their own pace.

Day one of week one was 'a focus on our customers' in which they defined three types of customer. Lucy hoped she wouldn't be found out but she was simply drawing on the experience of Mike, the life insurance salesman, blended with Transactional Analysis. Lucy still had his card in her pocket. It was a simple definition of customers but her colleagues were excited to be allowed to come to their own conclusion for once.

Lucy hoped they would realise that the current script permitted almost no emotional engagement. She knew that her colleagues who had come to the barn dance had agreed to do so partly because they had enjoyed the ticket buying process. In a similar way, if she could help her colleagues make the buying process enjoyable for their customers, they would start to question the validity of the current script.

As the workshops only kept her busy in the mornings she asked Robert for permission to do some market research. She got it easily and the words that Robert actually used were: "Young lady, we have been looking for someone like you to do this for us for years." This was better than a 'yes' because Lucy now believed that she would be permitted to make mistakes which meant that she could take risks – and that meant possibly upsetting a few customers as she learned where the edges of their tolerance lay. She didn't like doing it but she believed it was necessary to sacrifice a few to ensure the best result for most people; plus, she knew she could probably stop when they were close to being upset by listening closely to the tone of their voice.

What she wanted to know was whether her evaluation by emotional engagement had any relationship with the company's demographic target marketing.

It only took her a month of workshops to have everyone hungry to adopt a new process and by then, her market research had proved that there was no relationship between the company's target marketing and her own psychographic target marketing. She took her findings to Robert, who asked her to prepare a presentation for the board of directors.

Lucy was dumbfounded. In her wildest dreams she had never anticipated giving a presentation to any board at the age of twenty three – even twenty three and eleven months; but she wasn't going to let Robert think he was asking too much of her. So, even though she had a million questions to ask, she simply said: "Tell me more about what will be expected please?" It was a big question, perhaps too big with their limited level of rapport, but it worked; and Robert gave her a two hour initiation. He explained that he, too, had been the best telephone sales adviser in his day and had learned to loathe the script but didn't know how to go about changing it. Therefore, Lucy's formula was in great demand and the pressure was considered to be on.

"I am not going to let myself feel pressurised dad," she said. She had turned to the only expert deliverer of presentations that she knew. “Well, don’t be too relaxed about it,” he answered. “The nerves you feel are doing their job for a good reason. They are chemically enhancing you to perform better than you might otherwise do and you can easily re-label any fear you feel as excitement.” “But there are so many different people on the board with different attitudes to scripting and engagement. Is it possible to satisfy them all?” she cried. “If I told you, ‘yes’, would you feel any better about it?” “I don’t think I would believe you,” said Lucy. “Well, there you are; all you can do is present a balanced argument for your proposal and the alternatives but for your own piece of mind, state your commitment to the project so they can make their own conclusion with reference to your recommendation.”

So Lucy worked backwards from the premise that emotional engagement made sales calls enjoyable for the customer, profitable for the company and sustainable for telephone sales consultants. She planned to wear her smartest skirt suit, her highest, four inch heels and plenty of makeup because she was petrified to be among large and powerful businessmen. She laid everything out for the morning and went to bed running through the structure for her presentation silently in her mind. Only when she could memorise each section of what she wanted to say did she allow herself to drop off into a deep sleep; but at four in the morning she woke with a start. “This is really good stuff!” she thought. “And a well structured argument. I don’t need to dress up like a puppet.” And she went back to sleep only to be woken by her alarm.

Lucy looked tiny among the board members. She had stuck with her smart suit but she had chosen shiny black Snow White pumps and optimal makeup. She knew Jack and her dad would be proud of her. They let her go first and Robert gave her a wonderfully warm introduction so she forced herself to smile, and breathe through her fear; but she still had an out of body experience, looking down on herself, so out of place among the career decision-makers. Who was she to turn around the policy of a company, perhaps even an industry? “Well,” she thought, “I’ll soon know.” She had memorised the first few lines and was delighted to see that she held their rapt attention; so she relaxed and told her story almost completely.

They were as attentive as little boys at bedtime and couldn't avoid the obvious conclusion that customers should come first during a sales call; so they voted to give Lucy's Formula for Emotional Engagement a three month trial. She smiled inwardly – and outwardly. After all, who could avoid a call strategy that concluded with either 'yes, now,' 'yes, later' or 'yes, when something changes'?

AUTHOR'S NOTE

Lucy no longer stops thinking about work at five and she wants her colleagues to take ownership of their work too. She recognises that we are selling to each other all the time and the only way to improve our rate of success is to constantly analyse our own behaviour and that of our customers. The company has accepted that this process is the way to engage with the customers and have identified that their profitability, efficiency and role as trusted and preferred supplier for the future will improve as a consequence.

We say

"Ah!"

when we realise that we have missed something or made a mistake; but we know that it will only make us stronger.

16. Embarrassment

Lucy lay in her bed. She could consider getting her own flat now. It was lovely at her dad's by the sea but ideally, she would be nearer to the shops, cafes and energy of Bournemouth. Her life would start for real once she could make her own independent decisions and that is why she had taken the week off, to sort it all out.

The seagulls cried and the birds sang as she lay there, allowing the world to wake up around her. The company had offered her a permanent position with three months notice on an amazing salary. Lucy was satisfied and considered how lucky she was. Sure, she had worked hard but to be fit, healthy and well rested, lying in clean sheets, was a real privilege. The birds made her feel free and alive. They were inspiring. "That's a funny word, inspiring. What is it about birdsong that could be inspiring?" she thought. "I wonder what they are saying?" she asked out loud. "Well, they are not going to be wasting time saying 'good morning' or 'how are you?' It must be something more functional than that. It's probably, 'this is my patch,' or 'I'm hungry,' or 'is anyone in the mood for lurve?'"

"OMG, that's all it can be!"

She sat up. "So why do we like it so much?" How can we humans think that such a fundamental message is beautiful?" Lucy began to think about the interpretation of sound and got up. She poured herself a glass of orange juice. Glug, glug. "That's a lovely sound," she thought. "Why?" She turned on the television breakfast news at the adverts. A baby was cooing in her perfect nappy. "That's a gorgeous sound. It makes me feel....." she struggled to decide. "Content," she thought. Then an insurance advert grabbed her attention with someone scraping their fingernails down a blackboard. "Argh," she thought. "That makes me feel......" She struggled again. "Fear," she decided. "Why is it so hard to voice my emotions related to everyday sounds?" she wondered.

The phone rang. It was Jack. He was on a satellite phone from the middle of the Pacific so he had to be short because they couldn't afford to waste their limited resources on niceties. He asked how she was, congratulated her and showed interest in how her week was planned. She gave him a brief summary, thanked him for caring and then he had to go. Lucy stood there in her pyjamas, feeling embarrassed.

She had expected the call to make her feel good. Their conversations were normally a series of comforting sounds that didn't have any real purpose other than to reaffirm their allegiance and that call hadn't done it when she had expected it to.

The weatherman began his announcement and Lucy watched with interest for her week off. He was very factual. It often amused her how they packed so much information into such a short time and, occasionally, with great style. His voice was level, his diction precise and the pace was rapid. Lucy felt "relief." It wasn't going to rain and only Friday was to be hot and sunny. That meant she could get on and find herself somewhere to live without missing any good sunbathing weather.

There were plenty of properties on the market to rent and the internet readily gave her a list of agents with a good number of options. She called the first, with no plan other than to make a plan. The woman who answered sounded contemptuous of her calling. Perhaps she thought nine forty five was too early to be bothered with customers. Lucy's hackles rose and she went into business mode, making her voice slower, deeper and flatter. The woman took the point and put her through to an agent who specialised in the area Lucy was interested in.

John was pleasingly excited to receive her call. He told her all about market conditions, what to look for and which streets would probably suit her best. They had a cheerful chat and made an appointment for two that afternoon with an option to look at more.

The next agency was completely different. The receptionist was very cheerful, although she sounded a little dim, Lucy thought, and the agent was all matter of fact. He demanded many details about her current situation that reminded her how her customers must have felt when they suffered her script-orientated calls.

Lucy needed to get on, so she agreed to see a few flats at ten the next morning but she hoped she wouldn't have to do business with someone who made her feel angry. She made a few more calls and took note of the flats she liked, promising to call when she was ready to book appointments. It was lovely to be in the driving seat but she was amazed how many agents tried to make out that they were doing her a favour by simply taking her call. After three hours of this she felt emotionally drained so threw herself into her book and grabbed a sandwich before her meeting with John.

What to wear was on her mind and this conundrum kept dragging her away from the book. A simple cotton dress might make her seem a little dipsy, a suit might prevent her from receiving all the relevant information and casual wear might say that she wasn't serious; so she opted for the dress. "So what if they think I'm an airhead," she thought. "I'm not, and if they try to manipulate me they will have to use all their ammunition and then I will be in a stronger position." She added a soft pink cardigan and square-toed court shoes with a two inch heel. Her flat would be very important to her so she had decided to spend all she could afford on it.

Lucy didn't believe in looking backwards. Her attitude was that the company would be 'an idiot' to let her go so the only way she would lose her job was if she decided to leave, and her next salary would be more, if not equal. In the back of her mind, however, she would be happy to go back and live with her dad if it all went wrong.

John was clearly impressed when he met Lucy but she thought he might just be pitching her until he explained his moment of hesitation, saying: "I'm sorry, I had no idea that you would be so pretty, um, from the way you sounded on the phone." Lucy had to take a moment to think.

"Didn't I sound cheerful, lively and pretty?" she wondered. "Perhaps I have more to learn about myself," she mused.

He showed her a number of flats, one of which she fell in love with immediately. It had a balcony with a sea view, hardwood flooring throughout but a very basic kitchen and small lounge – perfect to her tidy mind. She enjoyed the process because John kept the sharing of information part light-hearted and fun, but he occasionally sounded serious when they had to agree what she did and didn't like. In her mind, she had found her flat and it was within budget; but it was a buyer's market so she promised to call him before the end of the week, once she had looked at her options.

The rest of the week was hell in comparison. She had been so lucky with John but the other agents were more interested in themselves, what she represented to them in commission and how they were the masters of her destiny. Lucy thought they were just a bunch of wankers but pretended to negotiate for a flat that was very similar to the one with the balcony that she loved. She found that the price was negotiable and went back to John on Friday morning. By the end of the day she had agreed a good deal as well as spending most of that day on the beach.

John called to re-confirm the deal at six that evening, as Lucy stumbled into her dad's place, all hot and spaced out. She was embarrassed about how she answered her phone but to be fair, in her mind, at six on a Friday, it was okay just to mumble "Hello." John didn't seem to care; he was clearly intent in asking Lucy out on a date. During their negotiation he had learned a lot about her and she had revealed, to her own surprise, that her relationship with Jack did not seem to have a favourable future. "And it's only a pizza," she thought, so accepted.

He was absolutely charming, but maybe a little too charming. It crossed Lucy's mind that he may even be gay and simply wanted her as a friend. He complimented her a lot and that gave her the confidence to be herself, so she teased him because he was clearly quite happy in his own skin, good looking and had a wonderful body.

Lucy realised that it had been a long time since she had really been able to relax and enjoy the company of someone of the opposite sex. He wasn't a wimp, either. He teased her back and she found that she could take it, absorbing some things that would normally have hurt her a little. She even expanded on her own weaknesses, recognising that she was quite creative, building scenarios in which she needed him and he needed her. These visions were, in effect, compliments to him and his relationship with her in the unknown future.

She went to the loo, checked her appearance, applied a little more lip balm and stood back. This circular flow of compliments, confidence and creativity was the key to enjoying sales.

AUTHOR'S NOTE

To Lucy, life is now just a bunch of sounds that affect her customers' emotions and therefore likelihood to like, do or buy something. She is beginning to see patterns in the sound that can be manipulated but recognises that liking, choosing or buying anything, should be a wonderful and emotional experience. The key to success, she concludes, is to believe that every opportunity is a good one until customer and telephone sales adviser agree otherwise.

“Ha ha ha.”

You have to laugh when everyone plays your game successfully and helps you look good.

17. Amusement

Lucy was really pleased with John. He had that lovely body plus, he was really into the philosophy of sales. He said that he 'sold through the customer'. "I didn't sell you your flat," he said. "I sold you the dream, experience and adventure it would bring to you, didn't I?" Lucy had to agree. Once the fundamental function was served she had taken the flat because the balcony represented dreams of being on the ocean, the compact lounge had represented close and meaningful relationships and the wooden floor stood for easy care and low maintenance. "If you sell like that," said John, "the customer gets to enjoy the buying process too. Didn't you?" Lucy agreed that she had but something in the back of her mind told her that there was more to it than this.

John believed that, currently, the worst purchase was insurance. "It's such a miserable, box ticking process," he said. He didn't mean it as an insult to Lucy. "The best purchase I have experienced is a bike," he said. "What type of bike?" asked Lucy. "A mountain bike with on and off road wheels, twenty-one gears, lightweight frame, disc brakes and SPD pedals with cages, too; but none of that was relevant you know. It was how they sold it to me that was interesting. You need a bike, Lucy; why don't you go here and see for yourself?" he said emphatically, handing her a scruffy business card extracted deep from within his wallet.

They had agreed that she would collect the keys on Friday if all the paperwork had been sorted out. Her company would give her a great deal on the insurance of course but she thought it would be very interesting to call for alternative quotes. At work, all their calls were recorded, so she made a loud call to IT, asking if she could have a copy of the recordings for her training programme. She did this because she was worried that the other trainers would think badly of her if they thought she was making personal calls at work.

John was right; buying insurance was a miserable process and Lucy felt as though she was on trial. The answering system warned her to tell the truth and that she may not be accepted. The bored operative (Lucy couldn't even use the title 'sales adviser') clearly didn't care at all, demanded answers and then, when Lucy was given a price, tried to bully her into deciding on the spot. The operative kept quoting what she thought were special features about the insurance and how much better her company was than the competition so that Lucy had to hand off each attempt like a karate master. In the end, she was made to feel guilty for taking their time and an idiot for not believing them when they told her it was 'the right thing to do'. "Phew," she thought. "John was right. That was awful." She arranged for the recordings to be emailed to her.

"I am going to lunch and I may be a while," she announced. Her colleagues gave her some reproachful looks, suggesting that this was not the done thing. "Good," thought Lucy. "I need to rattle some cages."

She had purposefully worn a hat, which was ideal because it was a little chilly for her skirt and skinny t-shirt combination. Her first stop was an electronics shop at the top of the hill and as usual, they were delighted to help. The young man apologised for spoiling her hat but Lucy knew it was necessary and, within the hour, she left with a tiny video camera concealed on her head, and a wireless recording device in her handbag. All she had to do to activate the camera was press one of the three buttons on the device, just like a modern car key. She bought herself a sandwich and directed her car towards the bike shop that John had recommended.

He was right again; they were really good. A little cautious at first but when they recognised her attitude to the process they cheerfully guided her through a world of improved stamina, strength, confidence and options. She left the shop with a better life at her disposal, a good feeling and a bicycle to be proud of. Interestingly, this last point hardly mattered. Back at her desk she explained her behaviour and to the consternation of her colleagues, started editing.

Over the next few weeks Lucy ran workshops in the morning and afternoon, playing the film and sound recording to her colleagues. The feedback was amazing. From the previous workshop, those who had identified themselves as directional and passionate agreed with Lucy that the bike shop experience was brilliant; but those who had identified themselves as logical, preferred the insurance call. They all talked for hours about the choice of words, pace, tone and timing and agreed that the initial cautious behaviour in the bike shop was a moment when the seller would identify what pace, tone and timing was appropriate.

Lucy now felt confident to introduce her own version of the script and people said that it was more like a map. Soon after, she started to receive complaints. "It's not logical," they said, but Lucy knew what to do.

She had been helping out at the language school at weekends, partly because she felt responsible for introducing a buddying scheme they didn't have but mainly because she liked to practice her Spanish. The students had a very different attitude to many things so she invited a few of the adults to spend a morning or afternoon with groups of her colleagues in a workshop she named 'perspectives.' The idea was for her colleagues to chat with the students about everyday matters and realise that their attitude to working, drinking, loving and even washing, may not be right after all. That really made them think and when Lucy stood in the middle of the main sales floor she could hear that it sounded different. It sounded more collaborative.

Robert came up to tell her that he was very happy and he had brought her a coffee, taking half an hour to tell her about the incredible difference her training was making to their results. "Plus, they sound like they care," he told her. "But there is just one problem," he added. Lucy gulped. She knew it. Why would Robert come all the way with a coffee just to tell her good news? "What is it?" she asked. "Well," said Robert, at least doing her the honour of looking a little shamed-faced. "We are suffering increased staff turnover, which isn't ideal of course, so would you look into it please?" Lucy had an inkling that she knew what the problem was. She promised that she would find out and report to him as soon as possible.

Lucy now played club tennis on a Saturday afternoon. She wasn't very good butalways enjoyed trying hard and learning and although her club was always bottom of the league, some of the players were pretty good. They just didn't have the winning spirit, preferring a nice game – which suited Lucy up to a point.

It was a sunny afternoon and all the regulars were out. Bernard soon organised everyone to his own satisfaction but most were pleased just to be getting on. Lucy ended up with a group of other new members who were nervous and very unused to the felt surface and environment. The game was scrappy, the serves weak and there were a lot of trick shots being played. Lucy won a set 6-1 with Tony, who was a master of the backslice, but Lucy felt no satisfaction. Debbie and Peter would have been humiliated if they cared but they didn't, and Lucy felt as though her tennis had probably got worse, rather than better.

The other four finished soon after and Lucy partnered with Adam, who was a seventeen year old with a wicked topspin. Lucy felt as though she let her side down a bit; she was obviously the weaker player and Bernard and Tina capitalised on her weak backhand so she and Adam lost 3-6. Nevertheless, Lucy felt good. She had played to the best of her ability, and a little bit more to be honest, and was therefore pleased to have progressed her game.

Lucy cycled home and pondered the definition of winning. Perhaps more or less points were not the best measure of success; perhaps everyone optimising they performance was the best solution.

At work, Lucy interviewed Chris and Bryn who had both handed in their notice. She was a little worried that the new script and attitude towards customers was all too much but she was delighted to find the opposite. "No," said Chris. "It's exactly what I've been looking forward to hearing for years. Sales training never did quite add up in my mind. It seemed that we made sales by luck, or force of character. The former is very unsatisfactory and the latter makes me feel bad but you have shown us how to manage the situation and optimise the buyer experience profitably and I want to put this to work for me, running my own business." Lucy smiled inwardly. "So the training is 'too' good," she thought.

She had liked Chris from the moment they met. He was one of those people who are generous with their character and will always offer an opinion; but it is rarely more than an opinion. She was proud that he liked her training and happy that it inspired him to go it alone; but she knew he wouldn't have considered the hidden demands of administration, accounts and the irregular salary her dad often complained about. Plus, although he had confidence in what he had learned, Lucy knew there was a lot more to be taken into account.

She chatted about herself and her tennis so he relaxed, thinking that she was happy to let him go; but she wasn't. She felt a little responsible and selfishly, she wanted good people like him to test her next phase of thinking.

Wimbledon had highlighted the matter of grunting and screaming during a serve and scientists in Canada had proved that if the receiver couldn't hear the ball being hit, he or she couldn't estimate its direction, spin or power accurately.

"There is so much more to do and learn Chris and if you're not here, you will miss out on something even more valuable," she told him.

Chris and nearly all those who had handed in their notice agreed to reconsider and Lucy reported her results to Robert, who was pleased with her; but she didn't tell him that they were only staying for as long as she was delivering the training.

AUTHOR'S NOTE

Lucy has recognised that you cannot control people whether they be customers, colleagues or friends. Everyone adopts an idea at their own pace and in their own way. If you don't let them do that, they will take longer to accept it or reject it sooner. So, she presents her formula for Emotional Engagement as a map which is open to interpretation and allows her colleagues and their customers to adopt it at their own pace. Lucy has introduced Collaborative Selling to the company.

You might say

"aah"

as you tip your head back and prepare to help the other person take advantage of the situation too.

18. Contentment

Lucy's new neighbours were a funny lot. There was Frank, father of two boys with a young wife, who always seemed to be late. Frank would always say "Hello" cheerily and Lucy had tried to have a conversation with him several times, but he clearly wasn't interested. "Perhaps," she thought, "that is what engineers are like." Polly, Frank's wife, had managed to tell her the basics as she was rushing to the boys' appointment at the dentist early one morning.

Nick was a policeman and again, although very smiley, he rarely said more than "Hi, Lucy. Alright?" She had been there for two months now and didn't know his wife's name. She didn't even know if their child was a boy or a girl so she assumed that policeman liked to keep facts to themselves.

Then there was Fred, on the floor below. Lucy often bumped into him after her evening run as he was coming back all covered in plaster dust. He seemed a lot friendlier but Lucy was beginning to realise that people had set patterns of communication. She now almost knew his procedure for making tuna and baked bean sandwiches and the exact route to where he worked in London.

It was a little annoying, she thought, that people would get so comfortable in their system, but supposed she would do the same one day too – or, perhaps her system was one of perpetual change. She wondered if that would annoy them as much as theirs annoyed her. It didn't matter a great deal, she thought; at least they lived in a type of harmony and she supposed she could rely on them in a time of crisis.

John stayed at her's a lot these days, especially during the week because he could walk the short distance to his office. Lucy liked him a lot. They had great fun together and Lucy found she could talk openly with him; but deep down she still loved Jack, even though they had now agreed to break up several times.

It was Friday night and she and John were going to a house party. Lucy loved house parties because they were a safe environment.

Some rooms were noisy for dancing and many were quiet for conversation and you could take your own drink, which meant no queuing at the bar – which Lucy hated, and no high bar prices – which Lucy hated even more. She couldn't understand why people would sacrifice their free time to suffer too loud music which only meant that they had to drink, and therefore spend faster. She did, however, know a lot of people who didn't really have anything to say for themselves and she supposed it suited them.

In the kitchen, they were greeted by Neil. He shared the house with four other guys who worked in town and this was a joint birthday party for him and Kevin, who sold telecoms. The kitchen was loaded with beer, wine and spirits, the lounge was hammering out tunes and the garden was packed with smokers. It looked like a good party. Neil introduced them to several of the guys who he shared with but Lucy knew most people there anyway. John got into a deep conversation with Kevin so Lucy went off to investigate.

The boys had generously re-arranged their bedrooms into lounges with different themes. In a large green room a bunch of guys were standing around with cans of lager, practically shouting at each other. Lucy knew a few of them from work and she was greeted with lager cheers and big bear hugs. A can was thrust into her hand and her opinion was demanded on the poor performance of Liverpool Football Club, whose ownership was being fought over in the High Court. Lucy didn't know anything about football except the off side rule; she always thought it would be useful to know that. She had, however, heard bits and pieces about various bids for ownership of the club and she could understand how not knowing would affect the performance of any player; so she threw her opinion into the arena in as boisterous a fashion as she could muster. The boys loved her for it but it felt odd, competing for attention like that while wearing heels and a dress. Lucy soon tired of the high energy competition and moved on.

One of the bedrooms had a balcony which was packed, not so much with smokers as she would have expected but a slightly older set. Lucy saw Robert, who called her over and kissed her on both cheeks. He introduced her to his wife and another couple and explained that they were discussing the current round of government cuts and the proposed changes to child benefit. Lucy had an opinion because she considered that she paid a lot of tax and just because the government had got their sums wrong, didn't see why everyone should suffer. Robert's friend Nigel gave her a pitying look, and a series of facts about fiscal policy and macro economics. Lucy didn't listen but realised that while she had felt contented with the boys, shouting about sport, she now felt sad to be lectured on something that she couldn't do anything about. The members of the group, however, seemed quite content to tell each other 'how it was'.

She broke away as soon as she could and bumped into Kevin, the telecoms salesman. He recognised her and assured her that John was happily talking house prices with another estate agent. John, it seemed, had told Kevin a lot about Lucy's performance at the company and he was keen to have her opinion of how he sold telecoms. He asked her if she minded and although she did, she was impressed that he had asked, and gave him 'five minutes'. Kevin had tried cold outbound calls to make appointments so he could convert users of other services to his own; but he found that it was easier to call them for another reason, which often led to a discussion about his telecoms solution.

He had taken a position as marketing manager of a local business networking group so called primarily to invite local businesses along to that. The pitch comprised some details about the meetings but the essence was that if they came along, they would win a lot more business. Of course, no one really did but at least the idea seemed credible and gave Kevin good reason to ask about the potential visitors' circumstances. They often ended up exchanging facts and occasionally agreeing to consider Kevin's service.

Lucy asked about his rate of success and from his memory, it seemed that Kevin was closing around one in forty calls for himself. From what Lucy now understood about key performance indicators at the company, she suggested that he could do a lot better if he made honest calls. Not that she was saying he was lying; it just seemed wrong to make the effort to connect with a potential customer and talk about something else. So, she told him about audience-specific language and the sound of a good call; but she wasn't quite sure what that meant yet. He, however, seemed very happy and they agreed to talk again in the near future.

Lucy needed the loo and she didn't want to talk business all night. As she sat there, she couldn't help thinking about how the tone of a conversation made you feel. So far, she couldn't say that she had enjoyed herself at the party but so far, men had dominated her conversation. Perhaps that was the problem.

She poured herself a large glass of sparkling mineral water, added some blackcurrant and was immediately accosted by Neil and his friend, who were fairly tipsy by now. She handed them off with grace and went in search of female company. In a room, glowing pink and orange, were a number of girls sitting in a circle of white garden chairs. One of them, who Lucy knew from work, called her over and introduced her to some of the others. They all took the opportunity to say "Hi" to each other and Lucy was given a chance to talk; but she didn't want to dominate the conversation so made a cheerful statement and as soon as she could, asked the others what they were talking about.

A slightly older lady called Shirley half explained to Lucy and half reinvigorated their conversation about Stacey Dooley Investigates on the telly and consumerism. The room was split into two factions, but they were both determined to be positive. On one side they were appreciating her good work, helping stamp out child labour in the third world and on the other side, they were appreciating clothes, shoes and cosmetics. "They should be arguing," mused Lucy, "but they aren't listening to what each other is saying, just how they say it."

She felt excited to be part of a conversation that had a familiar pace, tone and timing but when it moved onto movies and Lindsay, who she knew, explained to someone what it was about 'Withnail and I' that she liked so much, Lucy noticed something amazing. Lindsay's eyes took on a distant look, almost as though she was disassociating from the group, like she had gone into herself. She was recreating scenes from the film in her head and was really enjoying the process. "What do you think, Lucy?" asked Lindsay, who had clearly come back to them.

Lucy was concerned to make the most of this opportunity. On the one hand, she wanted to fit in and talk about something safe, like 'Titanic'; but she was also a fan of the message embedded in 'Withnail and I' and at the same time, she wanted to shock them with a description of a scene from 'The Dreamers', in which the sister dared her brother to masturbate in front of her and their mutual friend. Lucy stood in front of the group wide eyed and in a state of paralysis. Then she decided to shock them with the bedroom scene and the feeling of release was immense as the girls oohed, ahhed and grimaced, as she recalled the details.

AUTHOR'S NOTE

Lucy is delighted to note that if you give potential customers the chance to access their own unconscious memories and make sense of what you are selling, they really enjoy the buying process. To make this process profitable, however, she has recognised that by giving the customer opportunities to develop severalinterpretations of what she is selling, she creates stress – which is easily relieved by her closing the sale. The customers are grateful for the emotional experience and pleased to have been relieved of their stress.

“Mwoa.”

This isn’t an emotion but Lucy does appreciate your attention.

19. Kiss

"Uuumm." Lucy lay in bed, breathing the clean, slightly tangy sea air, feeling warm and cosy under her duvet. The sun was filtering in around the blinds and John was snoring lightly

They would go to the cafe for breakfast later and read the Sunday papers but for now, she was happy with her thoughts. She knew she could do it.

She knew she could bring that high degree of satisfaction to a sales call, that feeling of reward when others are interested in your interpretation of events; and she knew she could keep Chris and the others at the company because once they understood how certain sounds would elicit relevant emotions in their customers, they would all be happier in sales and make a lot more money.

Life is an adventure and although Lucy felt that she was close to solving this riddle, something was telling her that she had only just begun. It was fun trying because, while others enjoyed the benefits of her efforts, she was happy to be optimising her own sales calls and banishing her inner robot.

AUTHOR'S NOTE

Lucy is an ordinary person like you and me but has recognised that she only has one life and a lot of that is spent at work. She is going to make the most of every moment by optimising her interaction with every human being; and by putting emotionally-enriched customers as her top priority, she will make a lot more money.